Can Amber handle the

The Blue Stars went into their positions for their group floor exercise. As the starting note came, Amber threw herself energetically into a series of back handsprings.

"Amber," she heard someone hiss. "Wrong way!" Out of the corner of her eye Amber saw Lily mouthing at her frantically from across the mat. Amber's heart sank to her knees. The rest of the Blue Stars were over on the other side of the mat!

Her mind racing, Amber did a handspring back into position, but now she had lost count of the music. "The ribbon!" Chelsea hissed. Twirling to the side of the mat, Amber bent down and picked up one end of her ribbon.

She started moving it through the air, but her arms wouldn't move fast enough. The ribbon flopped like a limp noodle, then slowly came circling down around her. Amber went into the last spin of the routine, realizing when she was done that she was too late. The music had already ended.

As soon as she saw her friends' expressions Amber knew that the routine had been a total disaster. And it was all her fault.

Amber on the Line

by Emily Marshall

Troll

Published by Troll Communications, L.L.C.

Printed in the United States of America.
10 9 8 7 6 5 4 3 2 1

"Amber, keep your legs tight. You're wobbling," shouted Mrs. Randall, the coach of the Tillman Avenue Gym Club Gymnastics Team. Amber Rogers struggled to steady herself. She was on the uneven parallel bars, practicing a new handstand pirouette move.

The move was especially hard. Amber had to do a handstand, then switch the position of her hands to make a complete turn. She had been practicing the move for weeks, but hadn't nailed it yet. Something always went wrong. Either she moved her hands too slowly, or she lost control of her legs. Sometimes she didn't complete her pirouette quickly enough.

This time, though, Amber was determined to get the move right. She stretched her legs as far over her head as she could. Ignoring the stinging of her hands, she focused all her energy on keeping her legs straight and steady. Rapidly switching her hand position, she went into her pirouette. For a moment, she thought she was going to lose control. Then she finished her turn, and realized with a rush of exhilaration that her hands, arms, and legs were all in the right positions.

"You did it!" Mrs. Randall exclaimed, sounding almost as happy as Amber felt. "Terrific, Amber. You can come down now."

Her eyes shining, Amber quickly swung down onto the mat. "Way to go, Rogers," shouted Chelsea Higa. Chelsea was Amber's best friend on the team. She was also her spotter. That meant that Chelsea stood beside Amber through her routines, ready to catch her in case she fell.

"You were awesome," chimed in pretty, slender Lily Jackson. "You looked like an Olympic gymnast."

Their team captain, Jessica Knowles, pushed her smooth blond ponytail over her shoulder. "Yeah, you did well," she said in her cool-sounding voice. "Keep it up, Amber, and you might get as good as I am one day!" It took Amber a moment to realize that Jessica was joking. Amber considered all her teammates good friends, but Jessica still scared her a little.

"Thanks," she said eagerly.

Jessica shrugged. "Don't thank me. You were good."

"Yes," agreed Mrs. Randall. "I'd like you to hold your legs a little steadier next time. Other than that, you're definitely on the right track. You did a fantastic job up there, Amber."

A smile slid across Amber's face. Mrs. Randall hardly ever praised her like that. In fact, sometimes when Amber thought she was doing really well, her coach would surprise her with tons of comments on

6

all the tiny little things she was doing wrong. That was okay, though. A good coach had to be critical—at least some of the time.

Amber had taken gymnastics since second grade, but she'd only gotten really serious about it in the last year. She'd only been a member of the Tillman gymnastics team for three months. Of course, that was as long as the team had existed.

The Tillman Avenue Gym Club had decided to have a girls' gymnastics team when Mrs. Randall came to work for them. Before Mrs. Randall had gotten married, she had been an alternate on the U.S. Olympic Team. Mrs. Randall had never actually performed in the Olympics, but she had won a bronze medal on the balance beam in the Nationals in 1984.

The gym club had held tryouts for the team at the start of the school year. Over two hundred girls tried out, and Amber had been thrilled when she'd made the final cut. When she was chosen for the team, she felt like the luckiest eleven-year-old girl in the whole world. Chelsea and Lily had been as surprised to make the team as she was. Jessica wasn't surprised, though. She had left a more experienced team to join the Tillman team and have the chance to work with Mrs. Randall. Amber sometimes wondered if Jessica regretted it. She was so much better and more polished than the rest of them.

The new team's official name was the Tillman Avenue Gym Club Girls' Gymnastics Team. Tillman Avenue was the main street in Amber's neighborhood.

It was also the name of the school that she and the other members of the team went to—Tillman Middle School. However, none of the team members—not even Mrs. Randall—ever called the team by its official name. Instead, they called themselves the Blue Stars. It was Chelsea who came up with the name. She said the Blue Stars was the perfect name for them because:

1. their official leotards were blue;
2. as everyone knows, blue is *always* the color of winners; and
3. they were all going to be stars one day!

Chelsea giggled when she'd said that. So did the others. The Blue Stars were not only the best gymnasts Amber had ever known, but they were also the best friends she'd ever had. The four girls balanced each other really well. Jessica was always serious and focused, while Chelsea was the opposite.

Jessica was an only child, but Chelsea came from a huge family. Jessica *did* have a sense of humor, but it was hard to tell sometimes. Chelsea, on the other hand, never stopped cracking jokes. And while Jessica always looked polished in her classic clothes, the only word for Chelsea's look was *wild!* With her waist-length black hair and her crazy (but fabulous) clothes, Chelsea looked more like a would-be rock star than a serious gymnast. But when Chelsea got on the floor, she was awesomely athletic and very daring. Amber secretly enjoyed watching Chelsea almost more than Jessica. When Amber saw Jessica perform she thought, *How perfect*. When she watched Chelsea, she thought, *How exciting!*

Amber also loved to watch Lily perform. Lily wasn't as athletic as the rest of them, but she more than made up for that with her grace. Lily had taken ballet for years and it showed. Even ordinary jumps and glides looked elegant when Lily did them. With her curly black hair, round, soft eyes, and coffee-colored skin, Lily looked beautiful and mysterious.

The Blue Stars were the first real friends Amber had ever had. Ever since Amber could remember, she had been too shy to make friends easily. At home she talked a lot, but at school she quickly became known as the quiet one. It didn't help that the other kids at school were a little intimidated by her. Amber was a great student. She always, *always* got A's. Part of the reason for that was that she studied hard. Without a lot of friends, it was easy to make time for homework. But now that Amber was part of the Blue Stars, she knew how much she'd been missing. Life was so much more fun now! Of course, her schoolwork had been suffering a little, Amber thought with a twinge of guilt. The outline for her big history paper was due tomorrow and she hadn't even started it.

Amber jerked herself to attention as Mrs. Randall clapped her hands, calling them together. The small, trim gymnastics coach brushed her copper-colored curls out of her eyes and flashed them all a warm smile. "That's all for today. Just remember what I told you about always staying centered. Imagine a straight line running through the middle of your body." Mrs. Randall's greenish eyes twinkled. "You guys had a great practice today. Keep it up and we may give Barnard something to worry about this year."

The four girls broke into cheers. The whole city knew about the Barnard Gymnastics Team. Barnard Preparatory School for Young Ladies was a fancy girls' school on the other end of Tillman Avenue. Barnard had tons of equipment and money and a fabulous gymnastics team. They had won the citywide championships for the last five years running. *Mrs. Randall must think we're really doing well to say we stand a chance against Barnard*, Amber thought proudly.

"I told you the Blue Stars were winners," Chelsea crowed as they headed for the locker room. "That was our best practice all year. How about going to Fifty-Eight Flavors to celebrate?" Fifty-Eight Flavors was an old-fashioned ice cream parlor on Tillman Avenue.

"Sounds great!" said Lily.

"Yeah, all right," said Jessica.

Amber hesitated. She loved ice cream, even though, like the others, she had to be careful not to eat it *too* often. But just then an ice-cream cone sounded perfect. The only problem was that she really needed to get home and get started on her history term paper outline.

The paper was their longest, most important paper of the year so far. That was why their teacher, Mr. Goldman, had asked them to do an outline. Amber's paper was going to be about Sojourner Truth.

She was someone not many people had heard of, but she was incredibly interesting—at least to Amber. Sojourner Truth was an African-American woman who was born a slave, but fought to win her freedom. Once she became a free woman, she became a famous speaker. Even though she'd never gone to school, she taught others about the injustices of slavery. Amber's mom said that she was someone who had made a difference, and that making a difference was what life was all about.

"I'd love to," Amber said regretfully. "But I can't. I've got homework."

Chelsea rolled her eyes. "Amber, you always have homework," she groaned.

Amber could feel herself softening, but she shook her head again. "Sorry, Chelsea. It's that outline for the history paper for Mr. Goldman. I haven't even started it."

Chelsea wrinkled up her nose. "Join the club," she said. "But it's not a big deal, Amber. It's just the outline, right? I always do outlines at the last minute."

"That's why you don't get A's like Amber," Jessica said. "But Chelsea's right. It won't be the same without you, Amber."

"Yeah," Chelsea agreed, pressing her advantage. "Plus you did so well on the bars today. You have to at least celebrate your great performance. Come on, please?"

Amber hesitated. "I don't know. I want to, but . . ."

"You've got to," Chelsea insisted. "For one thing,

Mrs. Bonetti's son, Jason, is working the counter." Mrs. Bonetti was the owner of Fifty-Eight Flavors.

"The one who's in seventh grade?" asked Lily.

"Uh-huh."

"Ahhh," Lily smiled meaningfully.

"So?" said Jessica.

"Haven't you guys ever seen Jason Bonetti?" Chelsea exclaimed. "He is completely, totally. . ."

"Adorable!" Lily broke in with a giggle.

"Yeah, Amber," Chelsea said, nodding. "He's just your type."

Amber's cheeks felt warm. Chelsea was always talking about boys. She had a big crush on this boy, Doug Miller, in their class. Amber had never had a real crush. Even if she had, she didn't think she'd ever be brave enough to talk about it. "Chelsea! I don't think I have a type, okay?"

"Sure, you do," Chelsea said, sounding very sure of herself. "You just don't know it yet. So, are you coming?"

"Okay," Amber grinned. If nothing else, she'd be able to tell Chelsea her taste was way off. "But I can't stay long."

"Hey, I can't, either. I may not be a straight A student, but I've got to get some kind of outline in, too," Chelsea said. "Let's go."

The Blue Stars picked up their gym bags and strolled out of the locker room onto Tillman Avenue.

CHAPTER TWO

I guess he isn't working after all," Chelsea said in a loud, disappointed whisper. The Blue Stars were standing at the counter of Fifty-Eight Flavors. Behind the counter, a red-haired girl was waiting on a lady with two little boys.

"Bummer," sighed Lily. "Well, I guess we should just choose what we want."

"Yeah," Chelsea pressed her nose against the glass counter. "But I really wanted Amber to see Jason. He's so . . ."

Just then the swinging doors behind the counter flew open. A tall boy with curly brown hair stepped out from between the open doors.

"Ooops!" Chelsea covered her mouth. "That's him," she hissed, poking Amber in the ribs.

With a wide smile, the boy leaned over the counter. "Can I help you?" he asked, looking right at Amber.

"Ummm, yeah, just a minute," Amber mumbled. She hated to admit it, but Chelsea was right. Jason Bonetti was gorgeous!

"I'll have a single scoop of vanilla in a sugar cone," Jessica said firmly.

"I'll have raspberry cheesecake," Chelsea decided.

"Peach melba for me," piped up Lily.

Jason's eyes moved over to Amber. She noticed that his eyes were brown with tiny flecks of bright green in them. "How about you?" he asked. He had a really nice voice—deep and friendly sounding.

"Umm, chocolate peanut butter, please," Amber replied in a tiny whisper. She felt like an idiot, but she couldn't help it. Her voice always got really soft when she was nervous. She waited for Jason Bonetti to ask her to please speak up. People in stores and teachers at school had been saying that to Amber for as long as she could remember.

But Jason Bonetti surprised her. He only nodded and said, "Let me see if I got that. Chocolate peanut butter, right?"

Amber smiled. "Right."

She watched as Jason handed Jessica her cone. He chose another cone and started scooping out an extra-big scoop of raspberry cheesecake for Chelsea. He was not only cute, Amber decided, but he was also nice. If she did have a type, Jason Bonetti would definitely be it!

Jason handed Lily her cone. He was giving them all extra-big scoops, Amber noticed.

"Here you go, chocolate peanut butter."

Amber blushed. Jason Bonetti had given her the biggest cone of all. Her stomach did a tiny flip-flop.

"Uhhh, thanks," she stammered as she and the other Blue Stars paid for their cones.

"You're welcome," Jason grinned. "So are you guys on the soccer team or something?" he asked, gesturing at their gym bags.

"No way," Chelsea answered proudly. "We're the Blue Stars!"

"The what?"

"We're the Tillman Gym Club Girls' Gymnastics Team," Jessica explained.

"Wow. You mean you guys do headstands and back flips and tumbles and stuff?"

"You got it," Lily replied cheerfully.

"Well, I hope I get to see you guys in action sometime," Jason said.

"So do we," said Chelsea.

Jessica rolled her eyes. "Chelsea!"

Amber's cheeks suddenly felt hot. She tugged at Chelsea's arm. "Come on," she said pleadingly. "Let's go get a booth."

The four girls headed for the back of the ice-cream parlor.

"Didn't I tell you he was incredibly cute?" Chelsea sighed as she slid into a corner booth. Amber smiled as she sat down beside her friend. Chelsea was kind of boy-crazy, but Amber knew she acted more boy-crazy than she really was.

"Well, isn't he?" Chelsea demanded.

Amber shrugged. "He's not bad looking." She glanced over at the counter. "Plus, he's really, really

15

nice," Amber added softly.

"Am-ber," Chelsea's eyes sparkled mischievously. "If I didn't know for a fact that you have no interest in boys, I'd say you have the beginnings of a serious crush."

"A crush? On Jason Bonetti? Forget it. He's in seventh grade. He's like a million years too old for me," Amber said, trying to sound as if she totally meant it. She looked around at her friends. All of them—even Jessica—were smiling as if they didn't believe what she was saying for a minute. "I'm serious," she repeated. Yet before she could help herself, the corners of her mouth turned up.

"You do. I knew it," Chelsea squealed.

"Chelsea, lay off, okay?"

"Yeah," growled Jessica, coming to Amber's rescue. "Enough about Jason already. I thought you said at practice that you had a new issue of *Snazzy*. Is there another quiz for us to take?"

"Oh, yeah, I almost forgot." Chelsea pulled the magazine out of her backpack. "They have a really great quiz this week."

Chelsea held up the magazine. Inside was a photo of two girls. One was wearing a blazer and carrying a huge stack of schoolbooks. The other was dressed in a baseball uniform with a baseball bat slung over her shoulder. Above in big letters it said, "Brain or Brawn? How well-rounded are you? Take this simple *Snazzy* quiz and find out!"

"How can you not ace it, Amber?" Chelsea went

on. "You're a straight A student and a great gymnast. If that's not brain and brawn, what is?" Chelsea solemnly spread the magazine out on the table. "Everybody ready?" Jessica, Lily, and Amber nodded. "Okay, here's the first question."

It's the start of the school year. You are choosing your activities. There is a great aerobics class being offered after school, but it will cut into your studying time. If you take it part time, you won't get to do the step aerobics section. Also, the part-time class meets on Saturdays, so you will have less time to enjoy yourself on the weekend. Do you:

A. Sign up for the class anyway? You can't possibly be too fit.
B. Take the class part time? That way you can stay fit and have time for your studies.
C. Forget it? Weekends are for having fun.

"A," said Jessica, taking a neat, catlike lick of her cone. "If you want to be a good gymnast, you really have to exercise."

"I think I'll take B," Amber declared.

"B for me, too," said Lily. She took a bite of her cone. She had already eaten up all her ice cream. Lily was a fast eater.

"That's the obvious right answer," Chelsea sighed, "but I'm going with C. If I had to use up my whole weekend, I'd never survive a week of school. Plus when would I have time to shop the sales?" The others smiled. Chelsea was one of the champion shoppers of all time.

Chelsea went through the next five questions. Some of them were kind of hard to answer, like:

Your great-aunt sends you a check for $50.00. Do you:
A. Take tap-dancing lessons?
B. Buy a great looking pair of black boots on sale?
C. Use the money to go with your friends on a weekend wildlife retreat?

Amber could see doing any of those things. She picked C, though, because she would rather do something with her friends. Chelsea and Lily both picked B.

"Jessica?" Chelsea prompted.

Jessica frowned, thinking hard. "A," she replied at last.

"Tap-dancing lessons?" said Lily in disbelief. "What do you want to take tap dancing for?"

"Because," Jessica explained patiently, "studying any kind of dance makes you a better gymnast."

"I want to be a great gymnast, too," said Lily. "But tap-dancing lessons are too high a price to pay. My mom made me take tap when I was in first grade. I hated it. I wore my tap shoes to school by accident once, and all the kids made fun of me. They called me 'Garbage Can Girl' because every time I moved, I rattled!"

The four Blue Stars laughed. Then Chelsea totaled up their scores. "Now for the moment of truth," she declared, reading out the results. Jessica had gotten the highest score.

"You are so focused, it's almost scary!" the personality description that went with her score said. "Being committed to a goal is great, but you don't have to be an Olympic gold medalist to be a worthwhile person. Learn to stop and smell the roses."

Jessica scowled. "I'm allergic to roses," she said as the others giggled.

"Don't worry, Jessica," Chelsea said affectionately. "They just don't know who they're dealing with. For one thing, you probably will win an Olympic gold medal one day."

Jessica's face cleared. "I hope so," she said softly. "But who wants to be scary?" She twisted her eyes and lips into a gruesome monster face.

"At least you didn't get what I did," Chelsea grumbled. "Listen, here's mine: 'You have a lot of energy and enthusiasm, but the key word for you is focus, focus, focus! Don't spread your talents all over the place. Remember, there's more to life than an endless whirlwind of fun and games.'"

Chelsea frowned. "My life is hardly an endless whirlwind of fun and games!" she exclaimed indignantly.

"What does mine say?" Lily demanded.

"You and Amber both scored the same," Chelsea said. "Actually Amber's score was exactly in the middle." Smoothing down the magazine, Chelsea read, "'Brain or brawn? You are lucky enough to have both, and wise enough to know the importance of having fun. The only problem you may have is

19

keeping all the different sides of yourself balanced. You can do it if you try because you are well organized and well rounded.'"

Chelsea grinned. "See, Jessica, we're the weirdos. They're the lucky, well rounded, normal ones." She stuck out her tongue at Amber and Lily. "I hate you guys," she said jokingly.

Amber laughed. "It's just a dumb quiz," she said. "Besides, I don't feel so well rounded."

"Me, either," piped up Lily. "And when I do, it's usually because I've eaten too much." She patted her stomach.

Amber laughed. Then she lifted her head and glanced over at the clock. It was 6:15.

"Oh, no," she gasped. "I've got to go or I'll be late for dinner. Plus, I'll never get my history outline done."

"Yeah, I better get going, too," Lily agreed.

The four girls scooped up their bags and headed out the door. Waving to her friends, Amber hustled down the street. She knew her dad would be upset if she didn't have her homework done by a reasonable hour.

Her father had made her promise that she wouldn't let gymnastics interfere with her schoolwork. *It hasn't—yet*, Amber reassured herself. But there was no way she was ever going to get the outline for her history paper done without staying up seriously late. Biting her lip, she darted across Tillman Avenue and turned up Cedar Street toward her house.

CHAPTER THREE

Amber unlocked the front door to her house and poked her nose inside. The house was full of warm, buttery smells. Her mother had been baking pies. *Apple and cherry*, Amber thought, sniffing the air as she ran into the kitchen.

She wondered what the special occasion was. All at once Amber gasped. Today was her Grandma Ida's seventy-fifth birthday party! The whole family was going over to her grandmother's house. How could she have forgotten?

Amber's mom had been planning this party for weeks. Grandma Ida's husband, Grandpa Henry, had died almost a year ago. The family had decided to make Grandma Ida's birthday a really special occasion this year.

Amber took a deep breath. There was no way in the world she could miss her grandmother's birthday party. But going to the party meant that there was no way she would get her history paper outline finished by tomorrow.

Her mother set the pie down on the windowsill.

"Amber," she said, taking off her oven mitts, "you'd better hurry and change. We've got to leave in five minutes. Wear that nice new dress I got you, okay?"

"Sure, Mom," Amber mumbled. She headed up the stairs to her room and quickly pulled on her new dress. It was a great dress—fire engine red and fitted on top, with a long flared skirt. It was a lot flashier than any dress Amber had ever owned before. Normally, she would have loved putting it on. Today it just felt itchy. Amber frowned at her reflection in the mirror above her dresser.

She really wanted to enjoy her grandmother's birthday. Yet she knew she wouldn't be able to forget about the outline she was supposed to have done. Mr. Goldman probably wouldn't yell at her all that much. He was too nice for that. But Amber could just imagine how disappointed he would look when he discovered his best history student hadn't even started her outline for the most important paper of the year.

* * *

Mr. Goldman pushed his glasses up on his nose. "Okay, class," he said. "Today we're going to talk about the underground railroad. Now, my first question is, was it a railroad?"

Amber fidgeted in her seat. It was Tuesday, fifth period, American history. She was dreading the moment when Mr. Goldman would ask the class to turn in their term paper outlines.

As Amber had feared, she and her family had

gotten back from Grandma Ida's birthday really late. The party had been a lot of fun, and Amber could tell that her grandmother had had a great time. She only wished that somehow she had managed to get home early enough to do her outline. It was the first time in Amber's whole school career that she hadn't gotten her homework done on time.

Amber peered up at Mr. Goldman and sighed softly.

Suddenly, Doug Miller, who was sitting next to her, nudged her elbow. Amber started as he slipped a piece of folded paper onto her desk. Hiding it under her notebook, Amber opened it.

"Hey, Amber," it said inside in big loopy letters. "Don't 4-get 2 Smile! Remember the Blue Stars are stars forever." Below that was a picture of a smiley face. The note wasn't signed, but Amber knew who it was from. She peeked over at Chelsea, who was sitting three aisles away. Chelsea wiggled her fingers and grinned. Amber couldn't help grinning back.

At the front of the classroom, Mr. Goldman was still talking about the underground railroad. His horn-rimmed glasses were sliding down his nose the way they always did.

Amber listened intently as Mr. Goldman read out loud some memoirs of ex-slaves who had traveled the underground railroad. He told the class that roughly seventy-five thousand people had made it to freedom through the underground railroad.

"Now, class," Mr. Goldman said as he closed the

book. "Here's the moment you've all been waiting for." He smiled to show he was joking. "Time to turn in the outlines for your term papers. Remember, this is just your outline. You don't have to follow it exactly in your paper. But if you have any problems or questions, now is the time to talk to me. Just come on up and drop your outlines in this box on my desk."

Papers crackled and chairs scraped as all the kids picked up their outlines and headed to the front of the room. Amber got up, too, and slowly shuffled toward the front of the room. Chelsea was just ahead of her, holding a single sheet of paper in her hand.

"Hey, Amber, where's your outline?" whispered Chelsea.

"I didn't get it done," Amber whispered back miserably.

Chelsea's eyes widened in surprise. Then she gave Amber a sympathetic look. "So that's why you've looked so bummed out all day," she murmured.

"Yeah," Amber sighed.

"Hey, chill out, okay?" Chelsea whispered in a rush. "Mr. Goldman's not going to be mad. He may be one of the world's worst dressers, but he's a pretty nice guy. Plus, you're one of his best students. Once he gets your paper, he's not going to care one bit about your outline being late."

Amber smiled at her. Chelsea might not be the greatest student, but she was an awfully nice person and a very good friend. "Thanks," she said.

She looked up to see Mr. Goldman watching

them. Most of the other kids had already returned to their seats.

"Uh, here's my outline, Mr. Goldman," Chelsea said, handing Mr. Goldman her sheet of paper. She suddenly didn't sound nearly as sure of herself. Amber couldn't help noticing that the page was barely half full.

Mr. Goldman looked at it and frowned slightly. "Great, Chelsea," he said, "but this looks a little short." He didn't say it in a mean way. He sounded worried, which somehow made it worse.

Chelsea looked down at her feet. "Uh, I know, Mr. Goldman, but . . . uhh, I'm going to do a lot more research before I write my paper," she faltered.

Mr. Goldman smiled. "Sounds good, Chelsea." He turned to Amber. "So, where's your outline, Ms. Rogers?"

Amber winced. "I–I don't have it, Mr. Goldman." Her voice was so soft that she could tell he had to strain to hear her. "You see I . . . I mean there was, uhhhh, sort of a family emergency."

Mr. Goldman stopped smiling. "Oh, I'm so sorry," he said. "Is everything all right?"

"Oh, yeah. I mean, yes, everything's fine. I just need a few extra days to finish my outline, that's all."

"No problem, Amber. I just hope everything is okay at home."

"Yes, yes, it is," Amber whispered. Then she turned and practically ran back to her seat. The bell rang just as she sat down. Leaping to her feet like a jack-in-the-box, she raced for the door, almost tripping over Doug Miller *and* Bill Adams! She didn't even wave good-bye to Mr. Goldman the way she usually did. She felt too guilty. She hadn't exactly lied. In a way, Grandma Ida's seventy-fifth birthday had been a family emergency—for her anyway! But telling herself that didn't make Amber feel any better. It was obvious from the way Mr. Goldman had acted that he thought there had been a real emergency. She also knew that if she wasn't usually such a good student, Mr. Goldman would never have accepted her explanation so easily.

"Hey, wait up!" she heard Chelsea call behind her. "I thought we could walk to practice together."

Amber turned around. "Okay, sure," she said glumly.

"Boy," Chelsea sighed, slinging her backpack over her shoulder. "Mr. Goldman made me feel so bad about doing such a rush job on my outline. It's always worse when teachers are nice." She made a face. "You know, sometimes I wish I was good at school like you, Amber. I'm such a lousy student!"

Amber looked at her, startled. Chelsea sounded almost as gloomy as she felt. "That's not true, Chelsea," she said. "You could get A's like me, if . . ." She broke off. She'd been about to say, "if you worked as hard as I do," but that was the problem, wasn't it? Lately, she hadn't been working so hard. "What I mean is, it's hard to balance everything," she finished awkwardly. "You have a lot of other interests."

Chelsea nodded. "Tell me about it," she moaned. "Exercise every morning, gymnastics practice every afternoon, exercise more every night. Sometimes I wonder how we stand it. It's even harder now that we're in the Blue Stars, but . . ." Chelsea's voice softened. "I don't know about you, but hard as it is, I wouldn't miss it for the world. I love doing gymnastics."

"Me, too," said Amber. It was true: she did love gymnastics. Being part of the Blue Stars was the best thing that had ever happened to her. If only she could find a way to make it fit in more easily with the rest of her life.

CHAPTER FOUR

I have some exciting news!" Mrs. Randall greeted the Blue Stars as they came into the gym.

"This morning I got a call from the regional gymnastics council," Mrs. Randall went on. Her eyes sparkled with excitement. "They're holding a regional gymnastics exhibition at the athletics pavilion downtown. Barnard's team was supposed to be there to represent girls' gymnastics in our area, but they had to drop out.

"Anyway," Mrs. Randall paused for a breath, "the good news is that the council has asked us to take Barnard's place. It's a great chance for us to perform in a competition and to see how we hold up under pressure. I think the experience will really help us prepare for our upcoming match against Barnard."

"Who's going to be watching us?" Lily wanted to know.

"That's the best part," Mrs. Randall replied. "There will be a really varied audience: school kids, parents, teachers, gymnastics fans." Mrs. Randall's smile got wider. "Plus, some of the best and most famous gymnastics coaches and judges on the whole West Coast!"

"All right!" Jessica whooped. "That's awesome, Coach."

"I thought you'd be pleased," Mrs. Randall said. Her face became serious. "Of course, this is going to mean some extra practice. The exhibition is next Wednesday. We don't have much time to get our program ready. How do you all feel about practicing an extra afternoon this week, and also holding a long practice on Sunday afternoon?"

"No problemo," said Chelsea.

"Fine with me." Jessica was grinning ear to ear.

"Yeah . . . I guess." Lily sounded a little less enthusiastic. Amber knew that Lily's dad was almost as strict about her grades as Amber's dad was with her. But at last Lily added, "Yeah, it would be great."

Amber hesitated. Mrs. Randall shot a glance at her. "How about you, Amber?" she said. "As I said at the beginning of the year, if the gymnastics schedule starts interfering with your schoolwork, I want to know about it."

Amber looked over at her friends. It was obvious that all of them—including Lily—really wanted the extra practices. In a way, Amber did, too. They'd all been working on their gymnastics so hard! Performing at an exhibition was the perfect chance for them to see how good they really were. The only problem was that the extra practices would make it even harder for Amber to keep up with her schoolwork. She already had some serious catching up to do—namely, finishing the outline for her history paper.

"Amber?" Mrs. Randall repeated gently.

Amber tried to smile. "Yeah, it's okay with me," she said.

"Great!" The coach was obviously delighted. "Now, let's get going and start our warm-up."

The four girls moved out onto the mats. Mrs. Randall started them with some splits. When Amber first started taking gymnastics, doing a perfect split had been hard. It had seemed like a really big deal. Now Amber thought it was as easy as breathing. She stretched her arms up and bent over sideways until her head was touching her left knee. "Take it nice and easy," Mrs. Randall said, as the girls bobbed up and down. "Remember, don't push too hard. Keep yourself limber."

Next Mrs. Randall told them to stand up and do some backbends. They arched backward until their hands touched the floor. Amber liked doing backbends because they really worked her muscles. Next, they did press-ups and push-ups. Amber was good at those. She had to be. To do the uneven bars, a gymnast needed great upper body strength. Then Mrs. Randall told them to "shake out." The Blue Stars shook their hands, arms, feet, legs, and necks as hard as they could until all their muscles felt totally loose. The girls always giggled during shaking out, because it made them look so silly.

"Okay, everyone loose?" Mrs. Randall asked. "Great! Now today, I thought we'd focus on our group floor exercise," she stated. Jessica nodded happily, but Lily groaned. The Blue Stars had been working on a new group floor exercise. It was a great routine, but everyone except Jessica had trouble with the ribbon sequence at the end.

The Blue Stars had chosen a great Pearl Jam song called "Jeremy" for their routine. The rule for gymnastics floor exercises was that the music used had to be played on a single instrument. Chelsea had found a piano score for the song, and Amber's brother, Sam, had agreed to play it for them on tape.

At first Mrs. Randall had worried that even just on the piano, "Jeremy" sounded too hip for a floor routine. "This is gymnastics, girls," she sighed. "Not rock and roll." But now she agreed that the music worked. The routine was going to be fabulous, if only they could get it right.

The first part of the routine went okay. The four girls couldn't seem to keep in time with the music and each other. Still, Mrs. Randall said they didn't look too bad.

"Now let's add the ribbon sequence," she commanded. The Blue Stars fetched their ribbons. They each had a different color. Jessica's was pink, Amber's was blue, Lily's was purple, and Chelsea's was black. Chelsea had wanted black because she said it was the most elegant color of all! At first the ribbons twirled around them cooperatively, but then Lily let hers slip. The next thing they knew, the four girls were tangled up in a big spider web of colored satin ribbon.

"Help, I'm trapped," Chelsea wailed. She flailed a moment, then tumbled into a giggling heap on the floor. An instant later, Lily slid on top of her. Jessica carefully unwound herself, while Amber just stood still, laughing helplessly.

Mrs. Randall was laughing, too. When they were all untied, she gave them a serious look. "That was certainly dramatic," she said. "But I hope we don't do that on exhibition day. Let's take it again, from the top."

The four girls nodded earnestly. This time they concentrated really hard and everything went smoothly.

When they finished, Mrs. Randall rewarded them with an extra-large smile. "That was terrific, girls," she said. "If you can do that at the exhibition, we'll be a hit."

Chelsea tossed her arms into the air and took a flashy bow. "You mean, we'll be stars!" she declared. "Ladies and gentlemen, the Blue Stars!"

"Well, let's not get carried away yet," Mrs. Randall said. She led the team over to the balance beam.

"Okay, Amber, you're first," Mrs. Randall called.

Amber hopped up onto the beam as Chelsea moved forward to be her spotter. Amber narrowed her eyes and sprang into action, focusing on getting every move just right. An arabesque into a split, then a forward chest roll into a cartwheel, and then a flic-flac into a forward somersault in a tuck position. Amber relaxed, enjoying the feeling of all her muscles working together to make something beautiful.

Then, as she was heading into her forward somersault, she remembered that she had a math test on Thursday. The extra gymnastics practices were going to make it really hard for her to finish her outline and study for the test, she thought anxiously. The next thing she knew, Chelsea's hands had come up to steady her.

"Hey, Amber, watch it. You almost went off there," Chelsea exclaimed.

Amber jerked herself upward. She'd let her feet get out of position. If Chelsea hadn't been there, she'd have gone right off the beam. "Whew!" she stood up, blinking nervously.

Mrs. Randall came over. "Take it easy, Amber," the coach said. "You almost had a nasty spill there. Always concentrate on visualizing where your center of balance is. Remember, keep your body tight. Hips square and stomach in. That way you'll always be properly centered. Now try it again," Mrs. Randall smiled encouragingly.

Amber nodded, feeling flustered. She couldn't believe she'd almost lost it like that. How many times had Mrs. Randall told them: "Ninety-nine point nine percent of doing well on the beam is keeping your balance."

This time Amber managed to get through her routine without making any big mistakes. Yet when she compared this practice with the last one, she still felt something was missing.

Last time she had felt as if she was making a great leap forward. Every move she made felt smooth and fluid. *Like flying*, she thought ruefully. But this practice, she felt all mixed up inside. There were too many different things going on in her mind. School or gymnastics? Brain or brawn? Shaking her head, Amber leaped down to the mat.

"Much better," said Mrs. Randall. "But you're looking a little jerky up there, Amber. You seem tired. Get a good night's rest tonight, and try not to let the pressure get to you, okay?"

"Yes, Mrs. Randall," Amber said. Chelsea leaped up onto the beam and Amber moved forward to spot her. She couldn't help wondering how in the world she was supposed to forget about the pressure. She was still puzzling over the question fifteen minutes later when Mrs. Randall looked at her watch and announced that practice was over.

CHAPTER FIVE

"Amber, you have to come with us!" Chelsea begged. The Blue Stars had just gotten out of practice, and they were all in a good mood. The extra practice had gone really well. Of course, they had all made some mistakes, but even Mrs. Randall agreed they were making terrific progress. "Please?" Chelsea gave Amber a pleading look.

Amber looked at her feet. "I can't," she said, trying to sound as determined as Chelsea. "I have homework."

Amber had turned in her outline for her history paper that morning. At lunch Mr. Goldman had handed it back to her. He said it looked excellent. However, Amber still had a lot of schoolwork to catch up on.

"We all have homework," Chelsea sighed. "But, Amber, you finished your history outline and Mr. Goldman really liked it, right? So it's not like you're behind anymore. Besides, this is important. I have some totally amazing news!"

Amber hesitated. Something about Chelsea's

voice made her feel excited and curious. On the other hand, their midterm reports were coming out next week. Also, she should really get started on her history paper. "Well . . ."

"Plus, you can say hi to Jason Bonetti!" Chelsea fixed Amber with yet another pleading look.

"Okay," Amber gave in with a smile. "But I'm not saying yes because of Jason Bonetti. And I can only stay for half an hour."

"Half an hour and not a minute more," Chelsea promised.

"Then we'd better get going," Jessica pointed out. "We've already wasted five minutes deciding whether to go or not."

Picking up book bags and gym bags, the four girls started down Tillman Avenue. Soon they reached Fifty-Eight Flavors. Mrs. Bonetti was working behind the counter and Jason was nowhere in sight. Amber couldn't help feeling disappointed. Then she spotted Jason standing on a stepladder, reaching for some clean coffee cups from a tall cabinet. When he saw the Blue Stars, he climbed down and walked up to the counter.

"Hey, it's the gymnasts!" he said. His eyes met Amber's. "Chocolate peanut butter, right?"

"Right," Amber smiled back shyly. "But I don't know if I want that today. I was thinking of something lighter."

"How about a frulatto?" Jason asked.

"A what?" cried all four girls at once.

Jason laughed again. "It's Italian," he explained. "A frulatto is a kind of fruit milkshake. It's got milk and shaved ice and fresh fruit in it."

"That sounds great," Chelsea grinned. "What flavors do you have?"

Jason looked up at the board. "Let's see. Strawberry, banana, watermelon . . . ."

Amber smiled. "I'll have watermelon, please."

"Me, too," said Jessica.

"Banana for me," said Chelsea.

"I'll try the strawberry," Lily said. "You can't get much more low fat than strawberry." She sighed, glancing longingly at a tub of rocky road.

While Mrs. Bonetti whipped up the frulattos in the blender, the girls paid, then went and sat down in the corner booth. "Jason Bonetti is always so nice to you, Amber," Chelsea declared. "Maybe he has a secret, passionate crush on you!"

For a moment, Amber wondered if it were true. But then she glanced over at Jason. He was smiling and joking with a new customer. She shook her head. "I don't think so, Chelsea. I think he's just nice."

"Yeah, you're probably right," Chelsea admitted. "Anyway, you have to admit he's a total fox."

"Chelsea, shhh!" Amber begged as Jason Bonetti came walking up with their four frulattos on a tray. Maybe he would never like her, but she didn't want him to think she was just a silly kid. Her cheeks felt warm as Jason set the frulattos on the table. Despite their strange name, the frulattos were just as delicious as Jason had made them sound. They came in cool-looking tall glass goblets, with maraschino cherries and paper umbrellas stuck in them.

"Pretty fancy," said Chelsea, slurping hers appreciatively.

"Yeah, I feel like we're taking a vacation in Rome or something," Lily declared grandly.

"It's already a quarter to five," Jessica said. "Come on, Chelsea. We only have fifteen minutes. Time to start talking."

"Okay." Chelsea leaned forward, making all the bracelets on her arm jingle. "You know how the seventh graders are holding a dance in two weeks? Well, Elisa Carter, the head of the dance committee, got in touch with me. She wants the Blue Stars to do a routine at the dance!"

"Wow, that's great!" said Jessica. "It'll give us another chance to perform." Jessica often said that the more a gymnast performed in front of a crowd the better she became.

Amber bit her lip. "Yeah . . . but . . . will the whole seventh grade be there?" she asked. The idea of performing in front of strangers was scary, but performing in front of all the kids at school sounded terrifying!

"Yeah, and most of the sixth grade, too," replied Chelsea "See, it's a sixth and seventh grade dance. Anyway, the dance has this awesome theme: 'The Year 2101.' Elisa told me they're going to decorate the gym to look like a dance club of the future. Plus, everyone is supposed to dress up in the clothes they think kids will be wearing then. The dance committee wants us to do a routine that shows what kinds of dances people might be doing in the year 2101. This band from the middle school called The Zoom is going to be playing, but Elisa said we could pick our own music. She also said we should include lots of fancy moves— handstands, back flips, stuff like that."

"This is great!" Jessica exclaimed. "Not only will we get a chance to perform in front of an audience, but we can also do some of our own choreography." Amber knew why Jessica was so excited. Floor exercises were Jessica's favorite event. If she ever wanted to win medals for floor exercises, she had to get good at working out really great routines for herself. Good choreography played a huge part in how successful a gymnast's floor routine was with the audience and the judges.

Still, Amber hesitated. "I don't know," she said aloud. "I've never even been to a school dance before."

"Neither have I," Chelsea confessed. "But I bet it will be a blast, especially if we're performing."

"Yeah, 'The Year 2101,' starring the Blue Stars!" Lily breathed dreamily. "Maybe I can get Chris Haskell to notice me." Chris Haskell was a seventh grader Lily had a crush on. She wasn't the only one. Chris was the star of the soccer team, and just about every girl in school seemed to be crazy about him. But he never paid any attention to sixth graders.

"How can he not?" said Chelsea. "So what do you say, Amber?"

"Maybe . . . if my parents let me," Amber replied

doubtfully. "But . . ." She looked down at herself. As usual, she was wearing jeans and a plain T-shirt. "What will I wear?" she wailed.

"No problem," Chelsea grinned. "That's the best part. If we do a routine, we'll all have to wear matching costumes, right?"

"Right," they echoed, wondering what Chelsea was getting at.

"So," Chelsea smiled jubilantly. "I'll design us some totally fabulous outfits. My mom has all this great fabric in her sewing room. I'm sure she'll let me use some of it. I bet she'll help me with the sewing, too." Chelsea was good at sewing, but her mom was a fantastic seamstress.

"Are you sure, Chelsea?" asked Lily. "That sounds like an awful lot of work."

"Of course I'm sure," Chelsea declared. "This is the chance of a lifetime. How often do wanna-be fashion designers get a chance to make fabulous outfits for their best friends?"

Amber felt a thrill of anticipation. She'd never had a dress made for her before. She smiled at Chelsea. "It sounds great! But don't make us anything too wild, okay?" she added, glancing at her friend's outfit. Today Chelsea was wearing a peasant-style skirt, with lots of different colored petticoats underneath. "You always look fantastic, but I'm not sure the rest of us could pull off your look. Especially me."

"Okay, Amber," Chelsea grinned. "I promise I won't be too outrageous. But prepare to dress up a little, okay? You're so pretty, but you always wear—"

"Boring clothes?" Amber interrupted with a sigh. She knew the jeans and T-shirts she favored weren't exactly Chelsea's idea of high fashion.

"Not boring," Chelsea replied kindly. "Just . . . ordinary."

Amber stuck her tongue out at her friend. "Thanks a lot." She snuck a peek over at the counter. Jason Bonetti was standing behind it, laughing at something his mother had just said. Her heart gave a little lurch. He was such a great guy! Of course, there was no way in the world a seventh grader like Jason Bonetti would be caught dead at a dance. Still, maybe it was time Amber stopped looking so *ordinary*.

"Let's get together Friday after practice," Chelsea went on. "Then we can start figuring out our costumes and our routine. We're going to have to choose some music fast."

"How about 'We Are the Future?' You know, that new song by Vanessa?" suggested Lily.

"Perfect!" Chelsea cried. "I love that song."

"It's good," Jessica nodded. "Vanessa even does a lot of great dancing in the video for that."

"We'll all think about some good moves we can do to that song," Chelsea said. "And we'll talk it over Friday. Maybe we could try doing some switch-leaps. You know—"

"Hey, Chels," Jessica cut in, tapping her watch. "We're ten minutes over our time limit. We'll figure it all out on Friday."

"All right. Maybe you can all sleep over at my house!"

"Sounds good," said Lily. "Anything to escape another evening of listening to June thump around her bedroom in toe shoes." Lily's sister was dancing the lead in her ballet school's production of *Sleeping Beauty*. Lily claimed that ever since June had gotten the part of the princess, no one in the family was getting any sleep. June did nothing but practice day and night!

"Cool. I'll ask my mom about having you guys sleep over, and let you know tomorrow," Chelsea said.

"Okay." Amber slung her backpack over her shoulder. "It sounds terrific, but I really have to go." She smiled at her friends and, waving, ran out the door.

As she dashed home, her mind was in a whirl. It was thrilling to be performing at the dance. But now Amber would have less time to get everything done that she needed to get done. Somehow, without even meaning to, Amber had managed to make her already tight schedule even tighter!

CHAPTER SIX

Everyone stand up and gather around me," called Mrs. Randall. Groans echoed from around the gym. It was the Blue Stars' Thursday afternoon practice. Mrs. Randall had just led them through an especially grueling warm-up.

"Ouch!" moaned Chelsea, rising to her feet. "Every muscle in my whole body is begging for mercy. I thought warm-ups were just supposed to loosen us up."

"*I* feel loose," said Lily. "So loose I can hardly stand!"

Amber had to agree. When she stood up, her legs felt as wobbly as two overcooked noodles. She noticed that even Jessica had broken into a sweat.

Mrs. Randall grinned. "I know you don't feel so great now, but in a couple of days, you'll really feel the benefits of a workout like this. Now get over here. I have some news."

The four girls staggered across the floor and flopped down around their coach. "Now," said Mrs. Randall. "Guess who is going to be at the exhibition?

Susan Cooper!" she exclaimed, not even waiting for their guesses.

The Blue Stars forgot their pain. "Susan Cooper!" they shouted. Susan Cooper was a member of the current U.S. Olympic team. She had won the gold medal in the Nationals when she was only fourteen—the youngest gymnast ever to do so. Now she was eighteen and the star of the Olympic team.

"Susan Cooper is going to be watching us?" Jessica asked. "Unbelievable!"

"Wow," declared Chelsea.

Amber smiled. She loved everything about Susan Cooper, from the way she wore her hair (braids looped back into a French twist) to the leotards she wore (custom designed with bright embroidery). Susan Cooper was also special to Amber because her best event was the uneven parallel bars—just like Amber's. "Susan Cooper is going to be there in person!" she cried.

Mrs. Randall's eyes met hers and the coach smiled. "Yes, Amber. Susan Cooper is going to perform. Then she's going to hold a question-and-answer session for all the gymnasts participating in the exhibition. You can even ask her for advice and trade secrets, if you want."

"I know what I'm going to ask her," said Lily. "How she keeps her ribbon moving during ribbon exercises." The others laughed. Susan Cooper had won a bronze medal in the Nationals for her ribbon exercise.

Mrs. Randall smiled. "You can ask her whatever

you like, but I thought you'd be glad to hear she's going to be there. In fact, I hope it will inspire you. Still, we have a lot of work to do, so we'd better get started." She turned to Amber. "Let's start with you today. Get up on the bars, Amber, and we'll see what you've got."

Amber nodded and leaped to her feet. The news about Susan Cooper made her legs feel a lot less wobbly. *From overcooked noodles to super-charged rockets*, she thought with a grin. She bent over to rub her hands with chalk dust.

She raced forward and caught hold of the lower bar. Chelsea was already there, ready to spot her. Amber swung back and forth, building up speed. Her muscles ached, but they felt stronger, too. She did a smooth straddle-kip glide to the upper bar.

"Not bad, Amber, but keep your toes pointed! Nice clear hip circle, but you're still not getting enough height. That's better, now the handstand. Don't forget to point your toes, and hold your arms steady. No wobbling!"

Amber struggled to steady herself. Her palms burned. So did the muscles in her arms. But remembering Susan Cooper, she fought to keep every part of her body stretched and make every movement crisp and clean. She switched her hands and pirouetted, coming down to the lower bar again in a big rushing swoop.

"Nice!" Mrs. Randall said. "Now go into your dismount."

Amber swung to the top bar and flung herself into a somersault. She landed with her feet firmly on the mat. She felt out of breath and flushed, but happy, too.

She looked up at Mrs. Randall hopefully. Amber could never tell for sure, but she thought she was getting better. Mrs. Randall grinned at her. "You're improving a lot, Amber. But you still keep forgetting your feet. If you don't keep them straight, you lose height in your swings and leaps. That's your main problem—keeping good height."

Amber nodded. She had only heard this from Mrs. Randall about a trillion times before. She wondered how long it would be before the coach's advice really sunk in and her body remembered it. Another trillion times? Still, she couldn't help feeling good as Chelsea came up to do her routine. Amber moved under the bars to spot her friend.

Chelsea was a born daredevil. She wasn't as accurate as the others, but she more than made up for it by the way she could just throw herself into the air. "As if she could fly," Amber murmured. It was that feeling of soaring high into the air, free as a bird without a care in the world, that made Amber love gymnastics so much.

Amber suddenly grimaced. She was far from being free as a bird. She was catching up on her schoolwork, but she was still behind. Last night she had gotten all her English homework done. But by the time she had finished it was getting late, so she didn't study for her math quiz as hard as she meant to. The test turned out to be extra hard, and Amber was positive she'd blown at least two problems on it.

She stepped forward, raising her arms as Chelsea flung herself into a reckless back flip. She totally lost control of her arms and legs as she came down, but managed to catch hold of the lower bar at the last minute. Amber was relieved. She wouldn't want to try to catch Chelsea, though she would if she had to.

"Chelsea, that was way, way off," Mrs. Randall scolded. "You were trying a Korbut flip, right?" Chelsea nodded. The move had been named after Olga Korbut, the first gymnast to perform it in the 1972 Olympics. It was one of the hardest and riskiest moves a gymnast could do.

"I thought so," Mrs. Randall said. "I admit it's a dramatic move, but you can't try moves like that without making sure you have the skills to pull them off. Now get up there again. And how about something a little simpler this time? Try a simple forward salto onto the mat."

"Okay, Coach!" Chelsea swung back up to the upper bar again. This time she didn't fling herself off into her somersault with quite so much abandon. But she still leaped high enough to make Amber's pulse race.

"Fearless Higa strikes again," Lily said as Chelsea dismounted. "Fearless" was their nickname for Chelsea. "It makes me feel jumpy just watching her."

Shaking her head, Lily went up to the bars while

Jessica followed to spot. The bars weren't Lily's strongest event. She claimed all that swooping around made her dizzy. She also wasn't crazy about leaping from one bar to the other. She said if she was going to leap, she liked to know that there was solid ground underneath her.

To be great on the bars, you really had to like flying, Amber thought, grinning.

Today Amber could tell that Lily was really trying to be freer with her leaps, but Mrs. Randall still told her she was clutching. "Your positioning is good, Lily," the coach said, "but you're still hesitating. Just throw yourself into it."

"I'm trying!" wailed Lily. But when she did it again, she did look a little looser. Jessica was next. As far as Amber could tell, every move Jessica made was just right, but Mrs. Randall said that Jessica was rushing too much.

Next the girls moved on to the floor. They were pumped up and excited as Mrs. Randall started the music for their group floor exercise. As the familiar tune filled the room, the girls got in place on the mat.

"One, two, three," Jessica counted off, and they sprang into action. But almost instantly, everything started to go wrong. Amber's first leap wasn't high enough and she landed off beat. Jessica rushed through her leap, so the two of them weren't moving in sync at all. Then Chelsea overshot a handspring and careened off the mat, landing in a painful heap on the bare wood gym floor. And when it came to the ribbon exercise part, Lily flubbed her hand movements so badly that she got all wrapped up in her long purple ribbon.

Mrs. Randall blew her whistle, something she hardly ever did. "Okay, gang," she said. "I think we need a little primal therapy here. Everybody, scream!"

The first time Mrs. Randall had asked them to scream, Amber had thought her coach was out of her mind. She had pretended to scream, but actually she hadn't made a sound. Today Amber had no trouble yelling. She screamed just as loud as everyone else. The walls even shook a little. When they were done, though, Amber didn't feel that much better. She still felt frustrated. Looking around at her teammates, she could tell they did, too. They started the routine again.

It did go better, but the Blue Stars still had trouble keeping time with each other. Mrs. Randall sighed when they were done. "That wasn't so bad, but it wasn't as crisp as I'd like it to be." She smiled wearily. "I know you're trying, girls" she said gently. "Don't worry. It's normal to get pre-performance jitters. Only you're getting them a little early. Anyway, that's enough for today. We'll start with the floor routine at our next practice. Now get changed, and I'll see you tomorrow. Same time, same place."

"Okay, Mrs. Randall." The four girls slowly filed down the hall to the locker room. They quickly changed out of their leotards and pulled on their street clothes.

"That wasn't a bad practice," said Lily doubtfully.

"Until the end," Chelsea said.

"Yeah," Jessica agreed glumly. "Our group floor exercise was a disaster!"

"Don't worry, we'll nail it before the exhibition," said Chelsea, trying to sound confident.

"We'd better." Jessica frowned. "But we really need to do a lot of work. Maybe we should have an extra practice at my house on Saturday. If we just work on the routine and nothing else for a couple of hours, I bet we'll really improve." Jessica looked solemnly around at the others. "What do you guys say?"

"Absolutely, definitely, positively not!" Amber burst out. She was thinking of all the work she had to do—especially her history paper. She looked over at Jessica timidly. It was the first time Amber had ever spoken like that to her team captain.

Jessica's blue eyes widened. "Well," she said huffily. "I guess you must be really sick of practicing, huh, Amber?"

"It's not that," Amber replied. "I just have a ton of schoolwork, and we're already having an extra practice for four hours on Sunday."

"Look," Jessica crossed her arms in front of her chest. "I know it's hard. I haven't been spending as much time on my schoolwork as I'd like, either. But if we really want to be good gymnasts, we have to make sacrifices. I think an extra practice might make a big difference in how well we do the group floor exercise. If we work together, I know we can whip it into shape.

And Susan Cooper is going to be watching us. I just don't want to blow it in front of her, that's all."

Jessica's voice vibrated with passion. Amber tugged at her braid moodily. Jessica had a point. It would be so great if they could do their routine perfectly for Susan Cooper.

"I don't know . . . ." she said.

"Why don't we all just think about it?" suggested Chelsea. "We're all sleeping over at my house tomorrow anyway. Maybe we can fit a practice in then. But we don't have to decide right now. We can just see how it goes tomorrow."

Jessica nodded slowly. "Okay. But I still say an extra practice can't hurt. You know the old saying—"

"'Practice makes perfect,'" groaned Chelsea. "Do we ever! Jess, give it a rest, okay? I ache all over. Right now, all I want to do is go home and take about a six hour shower."

"Me, too," sighed Lily.

"Yeah," Amber agreed.

"And now let's hear it for the Blue Star Warriors!" Chelsea whooped, throwing open the locker room door.

Normally, the girls all would have cheered and given each other high-fives. Today the Blue Stars just groaned as they followed Chelsea out the door.

CHAPTER SEVEN

Amber toweled off her wet hair. The Blue Stars had just finished gymnastics practice and were changing back into their street clothes. They were about to go over to Chelsea's house for their first Blue Stars sleepover. Lily and Jessica were still in the showers, but Chelsea was already dressed and ready to go. "Hurry up, you guys!" Chelsea yelled excitedly.

Amber set down her wet towel and pulled on her T-shirt. Today's practice had gone really well, but they still hadn't nailed the group floor exercise. Jessica was right. They needed to do a lot of work if they wanted the routine to go right at the exhibition. On the other hand, Amber felt even less like having an extra practice than she had the day before. For one thing, she had gotten her math quiz back.

Amber frowned, remembering her shock when she saw the B– grade. Eighty out of a hundred. Only one point away from a C+.

"Lily, Jessica, come on!" she heard Chelsea say beside her. "You can take extra-long showers at my house!"

Wrapped in towels, the two girls stepped out of the showers and started dressing. Amber quickly pulled on her jeans. She was looking forward to spending the night at Chelsea's house, but she felt anxious, too. Was the math quiz just the beginning of a big grade slump? She wondered what her teachers were going to say on her midterm reports.

Amber pulled on her jacket and picked up her backpack. "I'm ready." Jessica and Lily were all dressed, too.

"Wait until you guys see the pattern my mom and I chose for the dresses," Chelsea breathed as they started down the hall. "It's so fabulous, you're going to die. Plus my mom had this great fabric lying around her workroom. It's blue and glittery—perfect for the Blue Stars."

Zipping up her jacket, Amber followed Chelsea out the door to where Mrs. Higa's old blue station wagon was parked.

Chelsea's little brother Carl was sitting in the front seat beside his mother. "Hi, Chelsea's friends!" Carl called out as they got in. "Guess what? My mom made a special dinner for you! She made baked chicken, corn on the cob, and cake. Rosie and I helped. Mom said we were great cooks and . . ."

"Carl, calm down," Chelsea pleaded, covering her ears. "You're talking so loud, I can't hear myself think!" Chelsea said it was great being part of a big family, except when everyone started talking at once. Then she felt like she was going deaf!

As Mrs. Higa pulled into traffic, Carl asked Amber and the other Blue Stars a zillion questions about gymnastics and what moves they could do. "Can you stand on your head and spin around?" he demanded. "Can you do three somersaults in the air or just two?" He was still chattering when Mrs. Higa pulled into the driveway of the Higas' house.

After they ate, Mrs. Higa and Chelsea took the Blue Stars to Mrs. Higa's sewing room. The room was piled with dress patterns and bright bolts of fabric. It was easy to see where Chelsea had gotten her love of fashion. There was even a full-size dressmaker's mannequin in the corner.

"Mom, show them the fabric and the dress we made for me now, pleeease?" Chelsea begged.

"Be patient, Chelsea, I was just about to get it out." Mrs. Higa pulled a bolt of fabric down from a high shelf. It was a silky fabric in a shimmery midnight blue, with silver glittery threads running through it.

"Wow!" cried Lily.

"It's beautiful," said Jessica. "Plus, it's light enough that it will be easy to perform in."

"My mom and I designed a short dress with matching shorts that won't restrict our movements at all," Chelsea said proudly. "We combined a couple of patterns. Where's the dress, Mom?" she asked urgently.

"Right here, Chelsea." Mrs. Higa held it up. The dress looked a little like an ice-skating costume, with a simple fitted top, short swirly skirt, and matching shorts underneath. It did look futuristic, but also kind of like the dresses Amber's mom used to wear back in the sixties. Amber smiled. She had been afraid Chelsea would design something so "fabulous" that she would never dare wear it. But this dress was perfect! She reached out to touch it.

"Want to try it on?" Chelsea asked eagerly. "We're about the same size."

Amber chuckled. "Only I'm about three inches shorter!"

"Don't remind me," Chelsea wailed. At five-foot-three, Chelsea was the tallest of the Blue Stars. She was always praying she wouldn't grow anymore in case she became too tall for gymnastics.

"The height won't make that much difference," Mrs. Higa said. "Go on, pull it on over your clothes." Amber felt shy for a moment. Then she gently tugged the dress over her head.

"Ahhh!" she heard the others say.

"It suits you," Mrs. Higa said warmly. "Take a look at yourself." Amber peered in the full-length mirror on the wall beside the sewing machine. The dress did suit her. She could tell, even though it was only pulled down over her jeans. In fact, it made her look a little bit like Susan Cooper!

"Chelsea, Mrs. Higa, you're both geniuses!" she exclaimed.

"Yes," agreed Jessica. "Now we just have to come up with a great routine to go with our great costumes."

"First, I need to take all your measurements," Mrs. Higa said briskly, pulling out a tape measure. "So Chelsea and I can get the dresses finished in time for the dance."

When Chelsea's mother had finished measuring them, the four girls carried their bags up to Chelsea's room. Chelsea had a big bedroom in the corner of the house. She shared it with her little sister Rosie but tonight Rosie was sleeping in their older sister Connie's room. Mr. Higa had helped Chelsea carry the television up to her room earlier that day so the girls could watch Vanessa videos in privacy.

Chelsea hit the remote control. Vanessa appeared on the screen singing "We Are the Future." As she sang, she and her backup singers formed a chorus line, kicking their legs high in the air.

"Any ideas, anyone?" Chelsea asked.

"Definitely!" said Jessica. "You know that verse about a new sun being born? Maybe we can act that out. We can begin all kneeling together in a circle. When the music starts, we can spring up, and with a big burst—"

"—explode, like a new star," finished Chelsea.

"Yeah," agreed Lily enthusiastically. "Then we can slowly come together again."

"Sort of like how scientists say stars are born," said Amber. "It sounds awesome."

"'The Birth of a Star!'" cried Lily.

"The birth of four stars," Chelsea declared. "The Blue Stars! Let's give it a try."

They moved to the center of Chelsea's room. Jessica's experience really showed as she suggested specific moves they could make. But when the Blue Stars tried to perform Jessica's ideas, it didn't go so well. With the four of them flying every which way, "The Birth of a Star" looked like a big mess.

"It looks more like 'The Birth of the Blob'!" Chelsea wailed.

"Yeah, I don't see this being a big hit with the kids in the year 2101," Lily admitted.

"It just doesn't have the right form," said Jessica.

Amber nodded. Suddenly she had an idea. "What if instead of a new sun being born, we act out that other line about a shooting star?" she said. "People make wishes on them. And they're the only stars that look like they're flying," she added in a soft voice.

"Flying! I swear, Amber, you should have been born a bird," Lily joked.

Amber felt embarrassed, but then Jessica said, "I like it! Let's give it a shot." Soon Jessica was ordering them all around. Chelsea was to be the star. The other Blue Stars would be the flaming trail left as the shooting star crossed the sky. It worked a lot better than "The Birth of a Star."

In fact, the routine came together faster than Amber ever would have expected. It was strong and simple, but Amber could feel that they were on the right track.

"I can't believe this is going so well," crowed Chelsea.

"Yeah," Jessica nodded, then she frowned. "If only we could pull together our routine for the exhibition like this. You know, we really ought to practice our group exercise at my house tomorrow. I even have mats and everything."

Like a balloon popping, Amber's good mood suddenly vanished. She thought of her math quiz, and also of her upcoming history paper. "Jessica," she said pleadingly, "I have to spend tomorrow on my homework."

"Well, if you're serious about gymnastics—" Jessica began.

"Of course she's serious," Lily broke in. "We all are. But that doesn't mean we have to practice every minute of our lives. I agree with Amber. I need to study this weekend. I have to start spending more time on schoolwork," she added sadly. "I totally blew my last math test."

Amber looked at her. Lily was in advanced math, too. "So did I," she confessed. "I only got a B-."

"Well, I got a C+," said Lily. "Michael is really going to tease me." Lily's little brother was a total math whiz. "I can just hear him now." She imitated her brother's squeaky voice. "Lily, I can't believe you don't understand long division. It's soooo elementary . . . ."

"Come on, Lily. He won't say that," Chelsea said, laughing. "Michael may be smart, but he's only seven. Seven-year-olds don't use words like *elementary*."

"They do when they're certified know-it-all geniuses," said Lily darkly. "The thing is," she went on, her voice becoming more serious, "I should have done better. I know that stuff."

"Yeah, well, I should do better in everything in school," Chelsea moaned. "At least, according to my mom and my dad. I even messed up that little weekly vocabulary quiz Mr. Goldman gave us this morning. I couldn't remember what half the words meant. Like *procrastinate*. What does that mean again?"

"To delay or put off doing something," Amber replied. "I should know. I've been doing a lot of procrastinating lately."

Jessica was silent a moment. "I understand it's hard," she said at last. "But we only need to practice for an hour or so. Getting everything done is just a matter of being organized. What we all need to do is make schedules."

"What good will that do?" Lily demanded.

"A schedule will help you see how much you need to get done, and how much free time you really have," Jessica explained. "Do you have any paper, Chelsea?"

"Yeah, sure." Chelsea went and fetched a notebook and gave it to Jessica. Jessica tore out a sheet of lined paper for each of them. Then she asked Chelsea to give everyone a pen.

"All right, now all you have to do is write down everything you have to get done in the next week. Then make a chart of your week, with everything marked down that you have scheduled for each day."

Jessica held up her sheet. She had drawn a neat box, with "Weekly Schedule" written on top and a column for each day of the week. The others quickly did the same.

"Okay," said Jessica. "Now that you've filled it in, look at your free time and figure out the best time to do all your schoolwork. Then you'll know how much free time you have left over."

Biting her lip, Amber filled in her weekly schedule. Then she glanced over the list of things she had to get done next week. She had another math quiz, an English book report, her weekly vocabulary quiz, and last (but not at all least), her big history paper. She looked over her free time. If she was strict with herself, she could get everything done. But it wasn't going to be easy. Then Amber noticed something that made her heart sink. Her history paper was due the very same day as the gymnastics exhibition!

"See?" said Jessica. "Doesn't that make everything clearer? I'll tell you what. Why don't we wake up extra early tomorrow and go to my house after breakfast? We can practice for an hour or two and still have the whole afternoon free to do homework."

"Okay, I guess," said Lily hesitantly.

"Yeah," Chelsea nodded. "Only I hate getting up early."

"And it's already late," Amber groaned.

"Then we'd better go to bed now," said Jessica. "I'll just go brush my teeth." She scooped up her perfectly packed overnight bag and swept out of the room. The other three listened to her footsteps pad down the hall.

"Organized," said Lily. "It's easy for her to say. Jessica Knowles was born organized."

"Well, I thought I was organized, too," Amber said, "but lately I haven't been feeling like I am at all! I always have so much to do. And there never seems to be enough time."

"I know what you mean," said Chelsea glumly. "But, Amber, you're so good at school. I'm one of the world's most mediocre students . . . ."

"Yeah, but you do lots of things well," Lily said.

"Like what?"

"Like design us beautiful, wonderful, perfect dresses," said Amber. She was rewarded by a broad smile from Chelsea.

Lily smiled, too. "Anyway, who knows?" she declared hopefully. "Maybe Jessica's idea of making a schedule will actually help us."

"Maybe," said Amber. She looked at her schedule. It did make things clearer. It made clearer just how organized she was going to have to be to get everything done on time!

CHAPTER EIGHT

We finally nailed it!" Jessica said triumphantly. "Our group floor exercise is going to look great!"

It was Monday afternoon and the four girls were leaving practice. They were all elated, with good reason. The practice had gone incredibly well. They had even managed to conquer the dreaded ribbon exercise in the group floor routine.

The practice on Saturday at Jessica's house had truly helped, Amber admitted. Somehow working on their own had made them solve their problems with the routine.

Plus, Jessica's idea of making a schedule had also proved to be a big help to Amber. Suddenly she remembered she had forgotten to cross off her book report from the "to do" list. She rummaged in her backpack and pulled out her schedule. She smiled as she crossed the item off her list. One great thing about having a "to do" list was how good it felt to cross things off it! A smile played across Amber's lips.

"What are you so happy about?" Chelsea asked her.

Amber shrugged. "Nothing." She stuffed her schedule back into her backpack. "I was just thinking, I'm really glad you guys are my friends."

"Well, we're glad you're our friend, too," Lily said.

"Yeah," joked Chelsea. "Where else would I find a Susan Cooper lookalike to model my fashion creations?"

Amber lowered her eyes in embarrassment. She had thought she was the only one who'd noticed Chelsea's dress made her look like Susan Cooper.

"Don't mention that name," Lily wailed. "I love Susan Cooper, but right now, every time I hear her name I get butterflies. I can't believe the day after tomorrow we're going to be performing right in front of her!"

"Yeah," Amber agreed. "I don't know if I feel excited or just plain scared!"

"Probably both," Jessica said. "It's normal to feel excited and nervous before an important exhibition. Anyway, don't worry. By the time the exhibition comes, you'll have been so nervous for so long you'll be totally used to it."

"I hope so," put in Chelsea. "Because if I get any more nervous, I'll turn into a big, blubbering mass of Jell-O."

"Chelsea Higa, the Jell-O gymnast," Lily hooted.

Amber laughed. They were passing Fifty-Eight Flavors now. She glanced longingly in the window. Jason Bonetti was there, zooming around behind the counter. He was joking and talking, the way he always did. Amber smiled, then she noticed her friends staring at her. "Wooo," Chelsea said, raising her eyebrows. "True love if I ever saw it. How about a quick ice cream, Amber? That way you can say hi to Jason!"

"Chelsea!" Amber pretended to glare at her.

"I'm only teasing. But doesn't a nice cold ice-cream cone sound perfect on a day like this?"

"Yeah," Amber sighed, blowing a stray hair out of her face. The weather had suddenly turned so hot that it was a record for this time of year. "But I can't. I've got—"

"I know, the dreaded H-word. Homework." Chelsea rolled her eyes. "Well, I guess I do, too. Okay, I have to turn off here. See you guys. And good luck on your paper, Amber."

Amber nodded. Then she said good-bye to Jessica, who was heading for the bus stop, and to Lily, who had to walk in the opposite direction. She whistled to herself as she walked along through the sticky heat. Despite the weather, she was in a great mood. Amber felt she was getting her life under control again. If she could get her paper finished tonight, life would be perfect.

"Hey, Mom, I'm home!" she called, pushing open the front door of her house. The house seemed weirdly silent. "Mom?"

"Not here," came Sam's voice from the kitchen. His voice sounded strange. Amber ran into the

64

kitchen. Her brother was staring at a note her mom had left on the table. "Oh, man," he said, shaking his head.

"What is it?" Amber cried.

"It's Grandma Ida. She tripped on her front steps and broke her ankle. Mom's taken her to the hospital, and Dad's going to meet them there. Grandma is going to come stay with us for a few days. Mom wants us to get dinner ready before they get here." Sam gestured at a package of chicken defrosting by the sink. Beside it was a bowl of potatoes ready for peeling and washing.

"Oh, no." Amber's heart sank. Whenever she tried to make plans, something always happened to mess them up! Then she felt awful. Her grandmother had broken her ankle. "Poor Grandma Ida!" she said aloud.

"Yeah," Sam agreed. "Anyway, I guess we'd better get started on dinner."

Amber took a breath. "Sam, listen, I have a whole bunch of homework to do. Do you think just this once you could take care of dinner and let me get to work. Please?"

"You want me to cook dinner?" Sam said in mock horror.

"Please? It's important."

"Listen, Amber, I would if I could. But I don't know the first thing about cooking. Mom's note says, 'Just shake and bake the chicken.' What does that mean? Shake it up before you put it in the oven or what?" Sam picked up a piece of chicken and gave it an experimental shake.

Amber sighed. "Sam, you're hopeless." Her mom had taught her to cook. She'd tried to teach Sam, too, but he always managed to weasel out of it. Her mom had finally given up. She said Sam would only learn to cook when it came down to cooking or starving. "Shake and bake means you shake up the chicken in some flour and salt and stuff."

"Cool," Sam said. "Where's the flour?"

Amber sighed again. Obviously the meal would never get made if she didn't stick around to help. "I'll get it," she said. "You just set the table, okay?"

"Okey-doke," Sam grinned. "I appreciate this, Short-stuff."

"Don't call me that! Besides, I'm not doing this for you."

Her brother shrugged. "Well, thanks anyway. And you're not the only one with homework, you know. I have a killer geometry test coming up tomorrow."

"But I have gymnastics, too!" Amber wailed, measuring out the flour, salt, and pepper into a large plastic bag. "And we have a big exhibition the day after tomorrow."

Sam looked at her. "Hey, relax, okay?" he said. "I know how you feel. Whenever we have a youth orchestra concert, I always get stressed out." Sam played first violin in the city youth orchestra. "I'm sure I'm going to mess up. Then I get through it, and

I don't even remember why I was so worried. Trust me. It'll be fine."

Amber hoped Sam was right, but somehow she didn't think so. The exhibition was bigger than a regular old concert. The day after tomorrow she'd be performing in front of a real Olympic champion. Only she had to get her paper done first.

Soon the chicken was in the oven and the potatoes were boiling. With the oven on, the kitchen felt like a steam bath. Amber let out a steamy breath. She wished her mom had come up with something cooler to make for dinner. In fact, she wished that tonight of all nights she hadn't had to make dinner unexpectedly. Frowning, she carried the salad she'd just made out to the dining room.

Sam had done a good job of setting the table. He'd even put out the good silver candlesticks. Amber felt a pang of guilt. He was trying to make it nice for Grandma Ida while Amber was just feeling sorry for herself.

Lifting her mom's best blue vase out of the china cupboard, Amber filled it with water. Then, armed with a pair of scissors, she slipped out to the backyard. Grandma Ida loved all flowers, but roses, especially yellow roses, were her absolute favorites. She said they were like pieces of sunshine. Amber hastily snipped a large yellow rose. She was just setting the vase on the dining room table when she heard the front door click open.

"Anybody home?" her dad called.

Amber and Sam ran out to the hallway. Grandma Ida was there, with Amber's mom on one side of her, and Amber's dad on the other.

"Grandma!" Amber ran up to kiss her.

"How's my favorite granddaughter?" Grandma Ida grinned. "Still doing lots of tumbling?"

"Yeah."

"Dinner smells great and the table looks beautiful," Amber's mom said. "Thanks, kids."

Amber looked down. "It was no problem," she mumbled.

"Look, a yellow rose," Grandma Ida cried. "How lovely."

They carried the food out and all sat down at the table. Grandma Ida declared that her leg didn't hurt all that much. "But I guess I won't be surprising my neighbors with headstands anytime soon," she said, shaking her head.

Sam laughed. After a moment, Amber joined in. "So what's new with the gymnastics team?" her grandmother asked eagerly.

Amber smiled. No one else in her family seemed that interested in hearing the details of gymnastics practices. Soon Amber was happily telling her grandmother about the upcoming exhibition and the routine the Blue Stars were doing for the school dance.

"We're doing a lot of switch-leaps," Amber explained proudly. "It's a really hard move. You have to leap up and do an aerial forward split. Then you reverse position so that . . ."

"It's nice to see you're so excited about gymnastics," her father broke in from the end of the table. "I just wish you were as excited about school."

Amber swallowed. "But, Daddy, I am!" she started to say.

"Amber," her father cut her off. "We got your midterm reports today. I'm afraid several of your teachers say they're worried about you. They say you've seemed distracted lately. Your grades are in danger of slipping."

"Charles," she heard her mom say. "I know you're concerned about Amber keeping up her grades. But I don't think this is the right time to talk about it, do you?"

Her father frowned, but he looked sorry instead of angry now. "Amber, I apologize. Your mother is right. This wasn't the time to bring it up. I'm just worried about your balancing school and gymnastics, that's all."

Grandma Ida reached across the table and squeezed Amber's hand. "Now, Charles," she said. "Amber is a smart girl, and I know she's going to be a great gymnast. She just needs a little time to figure everything out."

"I hope you're right, Mom," her father replied slowly. "But if being on the gymnastics team means Amber can't keep her grades up, then I think she should reconsider."

Amber bit her lip. Why did her dad always act as if her gymnastics was just a hobby? "Don't you see?"

her father went on, speaking to Grandma Ida but looking at Amber. "It's a choice between academics and athletics."

"Brain or brawn," Amber mumbled, remembering the quiz in *Snazzy*.

"Exactly," her father said. "And I don't have to tell you, Mother, that brains beat brawn every time. Gymnastics is fun for young people, but a good education will serve you well your whole life."

Grandma Ida's chin jutted out. "Charles," she said. "Believe me, no one knows as well as I do how important a good education is." She paused and smiled at Amber. "But you have to be a well-rounded person, and you have to do what you love, too."

Amber pushed her chair away from the table. "May I please be excused now?" she asked.

Her mother nodded, and so did her father. Grandma Ida smiled at her. "Bye, sweetheart. Now don't you be upset, okay?"

"Okay." Amber fled upstairs to her room. She shut the door and flopped on her bed. Brain or brawn? The words kept bouncing around in her mind like Ping-Pong balls. Why did balancing everything have to be so difficult? Her friends didn't seem to find it so hard. Of course, they weren't straight A students, either. Chelsea got lousy grades, but she didn't seem to care. Or did she? Amber remembered the worried look in Chelsea's eyes at the sleepover when she said she was the world's most mediocre student. Amber groaned. It was all so complicated!

She stood up and went over to her desk. Although she was feeling awful, she still had her history paper to write.

Amber opened her notebook to a clean page. "Sojourner Truth," she wrote across the top, "by Amber Rogers." Now what? She stared at the blank page in growing dismay. She had thought of a million things she wanted to say about Sojourner Truth. Now she couldn't remember any of them. "Sojourner Truth was a person who made a difference," she wrote. Then she stopped. She picked up one of the biographies of Sojourner Truth she'd gotten out of the library and started to read.

The next thing Amber knew, her mom was shaking her. "Amber, you fell asleep at your desk. Get up."

Amber sat bolt upright. "What time is it?"

Her mother smoothed down her hair. "Eleven-thirty, sweetheart. Time to brush your teeth and go to bed."

"But, Mom! I can't! I have to—"

"Look, Amber. You had a hard evening. Just go to bed and get a good night's sleep. Everything will look brighter in the morning, I promise."

"No, it won't," Amber murmured as she went to get her toothbrush.

CHAPTER NINE

Legs straight," Mrs. Randall called. Amber was doing a flic-flac on the balance beam. "Good. Now, go into your dismount. Try for more amplitude this time."

Stretching her legs, Amber went into her cartwheel. Holding her body straight, she flung herself off the beam, rounding off carefully as she came in for her landing. She hit the mat with a *thump* and looked down. Her legs were slightly bent and her toes were neatly pointed out. She had nailed it!

"Well done," Mrs. Randall nodded. Amber smiled and moved over to the beam to spot for Chelsea. "Okay, Fearless," said the coach as Chelsea leaped onto the beam. "Let's see your flic-flacs, and don't give me any flak!" All the gymnastics coaches loved to say this old joke.

Chelsea bounded into action. Her flic-flacs were great, as usual. Handsprings, even back handsprings, suited Chelsea's breezy athletic style. Chelsea had trouble with the round-off dismount, however. She made her cartwheel too wide and went off the beam too soon.

"Come on, Chelsea," Mrs. Randall groaned as Chelsea landed awkwardly on the mat. "Do it again, and please keep your legs straight this time, okay?"

Chelsea nodded. "Okay, Coach."

This was the final practice before the exhibition. The Blue Stars were so focused that they were practically giving off sparks. Even Jessica, who usually managed to keep perfectly still while the others were performing, kept shifting restlessly from one foot to the other.

"Chelsea really has to get more control," she declared, watching her teammate anxiously. "And a demi-plie should look more relaxed. Her knees look like they're locking!"

"Jessica, who's the coach, you or Mrs. Randall?" Lily said sharply. Amber looked at Lily in surprise. Lily hardly ever snapped at anyone. *She must be as nervous as I feel*, Amber thought. The practice was making her feel more excited about the exhibition, but it was also making her nervous. The Blue Stars were prepared, but they still had so many little details to get right.

Amber watched Chelsea try her round-off dismount again. This time, she looked much crisper. Mrs. Randall nodded, pleased. "Good work, Chelsea."

Jessica was next on the beam. At first, her routine looked great. Yet by the end, her nerves started showing. She performed her dismount well, but couldn't stick her landing position. She wobbled and had to step backward to keep her balance. Jessica made a face and scolded herself under her breath. Amber knew why. Not sticking your landing was half a point off if you did it in competition.

"Relax, Jessica," Mrs. Randall said. "You make it worse by tensing up like that. Remember what I told you. How you react to making mistakes is as important as whether you make them in the first place. Everyone makes mistakes, okay? The difference is that real champions know how to recover from them."

Jessica nodded. Then she got up on the beam and did her routine over again. This time she was picture perfect. "Ms. Perfect strikes again," Chelsea hollered, clapping loudly. Amber and Lily joined in.

"Thanks, guys," Jessica said, coming toward them. "But I really don't deserve it. I messed up my—"

"Jessica, for once, please don't tell us all about every little thing you did wrong," Chelsea moaned. "It just makes the rest of us feel worse."

"Enough chattering, girls. Get over here!" Mrs. Randall motioned them to the middle of the big old gym. "Now I want to talk to you a little before you go. I know you're thrilled and scared." Mrs. Randall's green eyes moved over each member of the team in turn. "That's natural, but there's one thing I want you to remember. This exhibition is only a practice. I know it doesn't feel like that, but that's all it is. It's the first time we're going to perform together as a team. Remember that and try to enjoy yourselves.

"Now I want you to go home, get a good night's

rest, and forget all about gymnastics. You've worked hard and practiced hard. As your coach, I think you're all more than ready." Mrs. Randall grinned at them. "So get up, shake yourselves out, and see you tomorrow."

That was one of the things that made Mrs. Randall such a good coach, Amber thought. Even when the pressure was really on, Mrs. Randall always spoke as if gymnastics was something to enjoy, not something to get all crazy about. Today Amber was especially grateful for that. She already felt pressured enough.

She slipped off her gymnastics slippers and followed the others to the locker room. Usually, they would all be talking a mile a minute, but today they were quiet. At last, Lily let out a sigh. "Ohhh, butterflies," she said, rubbing her stomach.

"Don't sweat it," said Jessica. "Mrs. Randall is right. We're ready. Now we just have to get out there tomorrow and do our stuff and be great." Jessica was trying to be reassuring, but somehow she made it sound like an order.

"What if we aren't?" Lily murmured.

That was just what Amber was wondering. She longed to ask Chelsea if she'd finished her history paper yet, but she didn't dare. Her teammates were already anxious enough. If Amber told them she still had to write her paper the night before the exhibition, they'd probably lose it.

She quickly showered and changed. Amber definitely didn't want to sit around talking or go for ice cream or anywhere else after practice today. Nevertheless, she was a bit disappointed when no one, not even Chelsea, suggested doing anything. For the first time since she had become a Blue Star, Amber felt really, truly alone.

"Well, see you guys tomorrow," she said at last.

"Yeah," Chelsea smiled. "And don't forget. . ."

"The Blue Stars rule!" Lily shouted as they all traded high-fives.

* * *

As Amber came in the front door, she could hear loud clattering and banging coming from the kitchen. Sam was sitting at the bottom of the stairs. "You won't have to help with dinner tonight!" he said, grinning. "Grandma Ida's taken over the kitchen." Amber snickered. Grandma Ida never let anyone help when she was cooking. She said it ruined her "cooking rhythm." Amber's grandmother didn't need help anyway. She was the best (and fastest!) cook in the world. Mrs. Rogers peered out of the den. "Your grandmother says dinner will be served in five minutes," she said. "So go on and get washed up."

"Where's Daddy?" asked Amber.

"Your father's working late tonight."

Five minutes later, Amber pulled her chair up to the table. Grandma Ida had made baked fish and a tossed salad. "Low fat, high energy," she declared. "Good for our gymnast!" Amber smiled gratefully. Everything tasted great. Amber tried not to eat too fast, but she still polished off her plate in fifteen minutes.

Sam had volunteered for dish duty, so Amber was able to get upstairs right away and start on her paper.

For the next two hours, Amber didn't even poke her head out of her room. She just worked. Finally, at 9:00 she slipped downstairs to get a glass of water. Her dad was sitting on the couch. "Hey, Amber, come say hi to me," he called.

"I can't, Daddy. I have homework," Amber replied.

"Amber sure has been working hard," Grandma Ida said quickly. "Ever since she came home, she's been hitting the books."

Her dad looked up from his paper. "Good," he said, and he winked at Amber. She didn't wink back.

Back at her desk, Amber stared down at her paper. The first few pages looked okay, but on the last few her handwriting had gotten really messy. Amber decided she'd better copy them over. First, though, she read over what she'd written. As she read, she scowled. Just about every single sentence seemed to begin with the word *then*.

Amber's fourth grade teacher, Mrs. Hauptmann, had taught her students it wasn't good to have too many sentences in a row begin with the same word. "It gets monotonous for the reader," Mrs. Hauptmann always said. Monotonous was a fancy, teacher-type word for boring. Amber hoped her paper wasn't boring!

She shook her pen and started copying. When she was done, she glanced over at her alarm clock. 10:40! She had to get to bed soon or she wouldn't be properly rested for tomorrow.

Someone knocked at her door. "Who is it?" Amber called.

"Me." Her mom looked in. "I brought you some of these peanut butter cookies your grandmother made today. She says they'll be good for your energy."

"Uh-huh," mumbled Amber.

"Shouldn't you get to bed soon?" her mother asked. "I know you have a big day tomorrow and—"

"I will! I just have to finish this up, okay?"

"Okay, sweetheart." Her mother shut the door softly behind her. Amber took a nibble of cookie and turned back to her paper. She had most of it done. It didn't seem like the greatest paper she'd ever written. Still, all she had to do now was write the conclusion. She looked over at the clock again. 10:45. She'd better write the conclusion fast.

"There are many interesting people in American history," Amber wrote. She paused and took another bite of cookie. "Sojourner Truth is a very interesting person. It is good to study interesting people like her because it makes American history interesting." Amber read over the paragraph. It sounded. . . monotonous! For one thing she had used the word *interesting* four times in a row!

"Knock knock." Someone was at her door. Again! "Who is it?"

"It's your father. I hate to bother you, but it's almost eleven-thirty. Time for bed. Remember, you have a big day tomorrow."

"How could I forget?" Amber muttered. "I know,

Daddy," she said aloud. "I'll be finished in a minute." She could tell her father wanted her to open the door. But she didn't.

"Well, good-night, Amber," he said at last. She listened to his footsteps shuffle down the hall. Then she leaned over her paper, and wrote "The End" in big letters at the bottom.

Amber gazed out the window. The houses across the alley all had their lights turned out. That meant it was late. Amber sighed. She had finished her paper. It was even going to be on time. Now all she had to worry about was the gymnastics exhibition. So why didn't she feel more relieved?

CHAPTER TEN

Timidly glancing around the arena, Amber sat down next to Chelsea on the team bench. She had expected the athletics pavilion to be big and intimidating, but she was still amazed by just how huge it was. Giant banners hung from the lofty ceiling. The biggest one said, "The 40th Southern California Girls' Gymnastics Exhibition." Below it a smaller banner proclaimed, "Welcome Susan Cooper, U.S. Olympian!"

"Wow! This place is gigantic," Chelsea whispered.

"Yeah," Lily agreed. "The only good thing is it's so big maybe nobody will see if we mess up."

"They'll see," said Jessica. She gestured up at a huge video screen that hung over the arena.

"We're going to be on that?" Amber exclaimed. Her mouth suddenly felt dry. She blinked—and yawned.

"Didn't you get any sleep last night?" Jessica demanded.

"Yeah, of course!" Amber replied. "Just not

enough I guess," she mumbled, half under her breath.

"Well, you should have gone to bed earlier," Jessica scolded.

"Quiet down, girls," Mrs. Randall said. "The exhibition is about to start." The Blue Stars listened as a voice announced over the P.A. system that the Woodrow Wilson Middle School girls' team would now perform.

Amber watched nervously as the Wilson girls took the floor. Next to Barnard, they were supposed to be the best intermediate girls' team in the city. In their sleek green leotards, they projected poise and power. The star of their team was a slim, brown-haired girl. Her style of performing reminded Amber of Jessica's.

As the brown-haired girl leaped onto the balance beam, Amber glanced over at her team captain. Jessica was watching the girl with a frown of concentration. Her hands clenched the railing in front of her so hard that her knuckles were white.

The brown-haired girl did a graceful aerial cartwheel, then went into a round-off dismount. She nailed it perfectly. With a perky smile, she waved at the crowd.

Cheers filled the arena. Jessica frowned slightly. Amber could tell what she was thinking. Here was someone who was as good at gymnastics as she was, and maybe better.

"Chill out," she whispered to Jessica. "You're definitely as good as she is."

"Yeah," Jessica whispered back. "But I don't smile that much, you know?" Amber nodded. "Samantha's always been good at that," Jessica added in a low voice. Amber's eyes widened. So this was Samantha. She'd heard Jessica talk about her cousin the gymnast a lot, but she'd forgotten Samantha was on the Wilson team.

Amber stifled another yawn. Boy, was she tired! Her eyelids felt heavy. So did every other part of her. She sighed softly. If only she hadn't had to write that stupid paper last night!

"Now," she heard the announcer say, "we are happy to introduce Ms. Susan Cooper. Let's give a big hand for our next gymnastics Olympic gold medalist."

The crowd roared as Susan Cooper came out onto the floor. Amber stared in surprise. Susan Cooper looked so small in person. Of course, Amber knew from her biography that she was only four-feet-eleven. But although she was small, Amber could see just by the way she walked that she was a champion. Susan Cooper's whole presence radiated grace and energy. Today she was wearing a white leotard with red and blue flowers embroidered on it. Her hair was pulled back in a simple French braid. Amber smiled. It looked a lot like how Grandma Ida had fixed Amber's hair that morning.

Amber was overwhelmed by Susan Cooper's daring. Watching her up on the bars was an incredible experience. Unlike Amber, Susan Cooper used handgrips. But using grips didn't seem to make it at all hard for her to feel the bar as it did for some gymnasts. She swung from the lower bar with power and suppleness. She did a beautiful kip-straddle glide to the top bar, followed by a Korbut flip. Then she quickly went into a handstand pirouette.

During her handstand pirouette, Susan Cooper held her body perfectly straight. Her legs didn't wobble even once. But it was the gymnast's next move that really set Amber's pulse racing. Without missing a beat, Susan Cooper did a flyaway double-back dismount in layout position. What that meant was that she threw herself backward off the upper bar and did two backward somersaults with her body straight. When she landed on the mat, her feet were perfectly positioned. It was so exciting to watch that Amber almost forgot to breathe.

"That was amazing!" she exclaimed.

"Yes," Mrs. Randall nodded. "There's nothing more thrilling than watching a perfect gymnastics performance."

Amber no longer felt a bit sleepy. She felt she would give anything to be able to do what Susan Cooper did—just once!

"Come on, girls," she heard Mrs. Randall say. "You're next." Amber leaped to her feet and followed the others out to the floor. As she went, she glanced around the arena. The place was so huge. She peered up at the gigantic video screen. *I can't imagine my picture up there*, she thought in a panic.

Mrs. Randall lined the four Blue Stars up in front

of the pommel horse. "Chelsea first, then Amber, Jessica, and you last, Lily," Mrs. Randall instructed.

Amber's stomach flip-flopped. Her muscles suddenly felt like they were made of lead. *Get a grip*, she told herself, trying to keep the image of Susan Cooper in her mind. Mrs. Randall was spotting for them today, so Amber stayed where she was as Chelsea got into position.

"One, two, three," Mrs. Randall counted off. Chelsea charged forward and did a handspring off the vault. She didn't quite get the height Amber knew she wanted, but at least she managed to stick her landing. Her heart pounding, Amber started running. Her footsteps thudded in her ears like doors slamming. Then she felt herself soar through the air. Her hands touched the horse for a moment and then she took off again. The ground met her before she was ready. She felt herself start to stumble, but she locked her knees and planted her feet firmly on the mat.

Mrs. Randall nodded at her. "Good job." Amber stepped back to watch her teammates vault. Jessica was great as usual. Lily didn't get much height, but she gained points by springing back off the horse in no time at all.

When the vaulting was over, the Blue Stars went over to the bars. Amber got in line, feeling as if she were on automatic pilot. "Hey, you're up first," Mrs. Randall motioned to her frantically. Feeling so tired she could hardly see straight, Amber rushed to the front of the line. Quickly putting chalk on her hands, she took a running leap and swung up onto the bars.

After watching Susan Cooper, she wanted so badly to be great. Her adrenaline surged, and her pulse steadied as the familiar movements of her routine took over her mind and body. Amber's upper arms felt strong and steady, her swings even and powerful. Yet as she went into her hardest move, the handstand pirouette, she lost her concentration for a moment. Her legs scissored above her head. She caught herself and finished. But she felt ashamed. She had wanted to be perfect, and she hadn't been.

Amber swung down into a backward salto dismount. It was a daring move. She'd had trouble with it in practice. Yet this time she performed it smoothly—maybe because she was too angry at herself to really think about what she was doing.

Hastily saluting the judges, she ran back to her teammates. "Nice going," Lily greeted her.

"Thanks." Amber tried to smile. The bars had really taken it out of her. Now her muscles felt heavier than lead. "I wish I hadn't messed up, though." She glanced at Jessica to see if she was mad, but Jessica was looking the other way.

In a daze, she watched Lily, Chelsea, and Jessica perform on the bars. None of them were at their best, but they didn't make any terrible mistakes, either. All in all, the Blue Stars weren't doing badly, considering it was their first time out.

Next was the beam. Amber blanched. She couldn't imagine how she'd get through her routine. The beam demanded great concentration. That was hard at any time, but now, when she was utterly exhausted . . .

She watched as Jessica leaped onto the narrow beam. Amber had to admire Jessica. She knew that watching Samantha had shaken Jessica's confidence, but you would never guess it to look at her. As she performed, Jessica appeared perfectly poised. When she went into her dismount, the crowd broke into loud cheers.

After Jessica's sterling presentation, the rest of the Blue Stars didn't feel quite so pressured. Maybe that was why none of them gave their greatest performance. Chelsea flubbed her forward salto but managed by some miracle to keep from falling off the beam. Lily's light, graceful style really had the crowd going until her dismount. She couldn't stick her landing and lost a whole half-point. But it was Amber who messed up the most. She was doing okay until she came to one of the simplest moves in her routine, a forward walkover. Somehow she walked over too far. The next thing she knew she went careening sideways off the beam. If Mrs. Randall hadn't been there to spot her, Amber couldn't bear to think about what would have happened!

She almost burst into tears, but luckily Mrs. Randall gave her a shove. "Remember, a mistake isn't the end of the world if you recover!" she whispered. Amber got back on the beam. She completed the rest of her routine without making any mistakes. But when she came off the floor, her cheeks were burning.

"I'm sorry, you guys," she stammered.

"It's okay," said Jessica. "You only lost half a point or so. We can make it up in the floor exercises."

"Yes," said Mrs. Randall, coming up behind her. "You've all done well up to now. Now just keep concentrating a little longer, and you guys will have given a great performance!"

Moments later the tinkling music of "Jeremy" started to play over the huge P.A. system. A bunch of kids in the audience starting cheering. "Yeah! Pearl Jam!"

Chelsea grinned. "I told you guys this was going to be awesome." The Blue Stars went into their positions on the mat. Just in time. In three more bars it was time to start moving.

Amber counted silently, "One, two, three." As the starting note came, she threw herself energetically into the first moves of the routine—a series of back handsprings.

"Amber," she heard someone hiss. "Wrong way!" Out of the corner of her eye, Amber saw Lily mouthing at her frantically from across the mat. Amber's heart sank to her knees. How in the world had this ever happened? She had gotten completely turned around. The rest of the team was over on the other side of the mat, and she was all by herself in the right corner!

Her mind racing, Amber handsprung back into position, but she had lost count of the music. "The ribbon!" Chelsea hissed. Twirling to the side of the mat, Amber bent down and picked up one end of her ribbon.

She started moving it through the air, but her arms wouldn't move fast enough. The ribbon flopped like a limp noodle, then slowly came circling down around her like a lasso. Forgetting to be graceful, forgetting to even try to look like a real gymnast, Amber untangled herself. She went into the last split spin of the routine, realizing when she was done that she was too late. The music had already ended.

Amber bowed along with the others, glad for the chance to hide her face for a moment. She straightened up slowly. As soon as she saw her friends' expressions, she knew that the routine had gone even worse than she'd feared. She glanced over at the scoreboard. The judges had already posted the scores. The highest score the Blue Stars had gotten was only a 5.0. The routine had been a total disaster! And it was all her fault.

"I don't believe this," Jessica said in a flat voice as the four girls walked off the floor. She glared at Amber. "What happened to you?" she demanded. Amber hung her head. She wanted to say something, but what could she say? Feeling tears start in her eyes, she picked up her bag. Then she turned and raced out of the arena toward the locker rooms.

CHAPTER ELEVEN

Amber sat by her locker, trying to control herself. She didn't want to cry, but tears kept sliding out of her eyes anyway. How could she have messed up so badly? She heard someone sit down beside her. It was Chelsea. Chelsea looked really upset, too. But she still cracked a smile as her eyes met Amber's. "Well, we weren't the greatest out there," Chelsea said.

"But it isn't the end of the world either," declared Lily bravely. She sat down on the other side of Amber.

"I guess not," Amber sniffed. "But . . . you guys didn't do anything wrong. I'm the one who caused a major disaster."

Just then Mrs. Randall came walking up. Jessica was with her. "Hi, girls," Mrs. Randall said. "I thought I'd find you here." She looked at Amber's tear-stained face. "Oh, Amber," she said. Amber gulped.

"Now I want you all to listen closely." Mrs. Randall's eyes moved across the four girls. "I know this a big disappointment, but as I told you before we came, this was a practice. There's a lot of talent on this team, but we haven't been together very long. It takes time to get used to competing and performing in front of an audience. It's easy to get rattled and make mistakes." The coach's eyes fixed on Amber. "Even on moves you know backward and forward."

Mrs. Randall smiled, then she sighed. "Believe me, I'm disappointed, too. But I've learned that when you have a bad day you have to put it behind you and go on. So let's not get carried away blaming ourselves—or one another. Instead, let's try to figure out what we can learn from this."

"I know what I've learned," Jessica said.

"What?" asked Mrs. Randall.

Jessica shrugged and looked away.

Amber wondered what Jessica had been about to say. Had she learned that she didn't want losers on her team? Another tear slid out of Amber's eye. She had learned one lesson for sure. Next time she had a big meet she'd make absolutely sure she got enough sleep. But then if she'd gone to sleep at a reasonable hour, she'd never have finished her paper on time. As it was, she had an awful feeling she'd done a lousy job on it.

"Amber." Mrs. Randall touched her shoulder. "When I said don't blame yourself, I meant you. Everyone has bad days."

Amber looked up at her coach and tried to smile. "Thanks, Mrs. Randall," she said.

"No problem," Mrs. Randall smiled back. "You're an important member of this team, and don't you forget it. Now I'm going to leave you guys alone for a while. Susan Cooper's question-and-answer session starts in fifteen minutes. See you out there, okay?"

"Okay," said Lily and Chelsea. Jessica just nodded.

Amber watched Mrs. Randall walk lightly out of the locker room, her coppery curls glinting in the light.

"Coach Randall always says don't blame yourself," Amber heard Jessica say. She looked up at her teammate. Jessica looked bitterly disappointed, but she also looked mad. "Sometimes you have to blame yourself, though." Jessica's blue eyes met Amber's brown ones. "Amber, how come you didn't make absolutely sure to get enough sleep last night?" she asked in an icy voice. "What's the good of doing all this practicing if you're going to fall apart when it counts? If you're going to stay on this team, Amber, you have to learn to stand up to pressure. Understand?"

Amber nodded wordlessly. What Jessica said made her feel hurt and angry, too. If only Jessica knew how hard she'd been trying! But maybe it didn't matter. Jessica was right: She had blown it when it really counted. Her tears coming faster, she glanced at Chelsea and Lily. Neither of them said anything. That wasn't surprising. Jessica was probably just saying out loud what all of them were thinking.

Amber picked up her bag, turned, and raced out of the locker room. There was no way she was sticking around. She didn't even care if she missed Susan Cooper's question-and-answer session. She just had to get out of there!

Suddenly Amber felt a hand on her shoulder. She looked up. Susan Cooper was standing right next to her in the hallway! Amber blinked. "H-hi, Ms. Cooper," she stammered.

Susan Cooper smiled. Her brown eyes twinkled warmly. "Hi, Amber. It is Amber, isn't it?"

Amber nodded, amazed that Susan Cooper knew her name. "Yeah. I mean, yes," she breathed.

"Well, Amber, I just wanted to say I enjoyed watching you out there."

Amber's jaw dropped. "You enjoyed watching me?" she blurted in astonishment. "But I'm the one who ruined everything!"

Susan Cooper's smile got wider and she laughed, a deep, rippling laugh. "Yeah, you didn't have the best day in the world," the Olympic athlete agreed. "But believe me, Amber, that happens to us all sometimes. I used to mess up something terrible when I was your age. Ohhh! I can still remember how awful it felt!" Susan Cooper laughed again. "But the important thing is getting out there again. It always takes awhile to feel comfortable in competitions." She looked at Amber. "How long have you been doing gymnastics?"

Amber swallowed. "Th-three years."

"Three years, huh? That's not all that long. You have a really nice line, Amber. And you have good upper body strength. On those bars, you really soared. You have real talent. I hope you keep working on your gymnastics. Now, would you like me to sign your program?"

Amber wiped away the last traces of her tears. "Yes, please!" She pulled the exhibition program out of her bag. There was a picture of Susan Cooper on the cover. She was leaping high into the air like a brave, beautiful bird. "Here," Amber handed the program to her shyly. "You could sign on your picture. Please," she added.

Susan Cooper pulled a pen out of the pocket of her warm-up jacket. She quickly wrote something and signed her name with a flourish. "Here you go, Amber, and good luck."

"Thanks!" Amber smiled at Susan Cooper as she walked away. Then she looked down at her program. On it Susan Cooper had written, "Dear Amber, I hope you will always love to fly, and remember, whatever happens, don't be afraid to keep on soaring (especially on the bars). Best wishes, your friend, Susan Cooper."

Amber blinked. It was the best thing anyone had ever written to her, and it was written by her favorite gymnast in the whole world. It was as if Susan Cooper had seen right into her heart and understood exactly what gymnastics meant to her. Maybe that was because Susan Cooper felt the same way about the sport. Amber clutched the program tightly, afraid it would disappear right in front of her eyes. Then she tucked it in her bag and kept walking.

"Amber, over here." She looked up to see her mom and Grandma Ida waving at her. They were sitting right up front.

"Hey, Mom, Grandma," she said. All the bad

things that had happened that day flooded back into her mind. "I guess you saw me out there. I really messed up, didn't I?"

Her grandma reached up and gave Amber a hug. "Sweetheart, you just made a few mistakes."

"I know you'll be great next time," her mom said.

"Come on." Her grandmother jogged her elbow. "I think we could all use an ice-cream cone. How about a trip to Fifty-Eight Flavors? That's the name of the place you like, right?"

"Sounds good," her mom agreed, then she frowned. "But Amber, don't you have to ride back with the rest of your team?"

Amber shook her head. "Uh-uh. I told them you were here. I'm sure they'll figure out I just got a ride from you," she mumbled.

"Okay, you take your grandmother's left side and I'll take the right. She'll need some help to get out of this place."

"Yup." Grandma Ida nodded. "If I fall down walking out of a gymnastics event, I really will feel like a fool!"

Amber smiled at her. "You won't fall," she promised, carefully hooking her arm around her grandmother's waist.

CHAPTER TWELVE

Amber curled her feet up under her nightgown and stared at the TV. For once, she didn't have any homework. Normally, that would have been a reason to celebrate, but tonight it didn't seem to matter. An old movie was just starting. Two tiny black-and-white figures tap-danced across the screen: Fred Astaire and Ginger Rogers. Amber reached for the remote control and turned up the sound. A lot of people thought old movies were corny but Amber loved them.

The phone rang from the hallway. Amber pricked up her ears as her mother answered. "Rogers' residence. Oh, hi, Chelsea. Hold on. I'll see if I can get her." Her mom poked her head into the den. "Amber, it's Chelsea for you."

Amber gave her mother an imploring look. "Mom, tell her I'm asleep. Please?"

Her mother sighed. "All right." She went back to the phone. "Chelsea, I'm afraid she's in bed already. I'm sure she'll see you tomorrow at school. Yes. Don't worry. I'll give her the message."

Amber turned her attention back to the TV. Fred

Astaire was clicking up his heels and dancing down a long spiral staircase. "Amber?" Her mom came and sat down beside her.

"Yeah?"

"I don't want to tell you how to run your life, but you're going to have to talk to your friends sometime."

Amber bit her lip. Chelsea's call was the fourth one she'd gotten that night. First Mrs. Randall had called, then Jessica, then Lily, and now Chelsea. Amber had made her mother tell them all she was asleep.

"I know you had a bad day out there," her mom went on. "But that's no reason to hide from the whole world. Your teammates are your friends. They're not calling to yell at you. They're calling to sympathize. Like just now, Chelsea told me to tell you she's thinking of you and not to be too hard on yourself."

"Chelsea would say that, but Jessica wouldn't," Amber muttered.

"What did you say?" her mom asked.

Amber sighed. "Nothing, Mom. I'll talk to them—just not tonight. Tomorrow, okay?"

"Okay," her mother smiled. "Now scoot over. *Let's Dance* is one of my favorite movies. Your dad's working late again, so I'll watch it with you."

"What about Grandma?" Amber asked. "Won't she want to watch the movie, too?" Grandma Ida had taken Amber to her first musical, and she was totally nuts about Fred Astaire.

"Well, she would," Amber's mother grinned. "But your grandmother happens to be fast asleep. I guess all that excitement today really tired her out."

"She's probably just disgusted with how awful a gymnast her granddaughter is," Amber murmured.

"Don't be ridiculous, Amber! You're so far from awful it isn't even funny. I know you made some pretty serious mistakes during the floor routine, but until then I was amazed at how good you were."

"Thanks, but you don't have to lie to make me feel better."

Her mother's face became serious. "Amber, I hope you know I would never lie to you to make you feel better."

"Sorry, Mom."

"That's all right. You're allowed to be crabby. I know what a hard day you had. There is one thing I do want to know, though."

"What?" Amber mumbled, fixing her eyes on the TV screen.

"You and I both know that you got into trouble today because you were overtired," her mother said. "I want to know why you stayed up so late the night before the exhibition."

Amber sighed. "It's sort of a long story."

"I have time."

Amber took a deep breath. "Well, I needed to get my history paper done," she said quickly. "I meant to get it done earlier. But we had extra practice, and then Grandma Ida broke her ankle. I just got a little behind, I guess."

Her mother nodded. "I thought that might be it.

Especially after what your teachers wrote in your midterm reports. You've always studied so hard, Amber, but you've never had anything else taking up your time. Keeping up your grades and being on the gymnastics team is turning out to be more difficult than you expected, isn't it?"

"Sort of," Amber said. "So what do you think I should do?"

Her mother shrugged.

"You think I should quit gymnastics, don't you?" Amber demanded in a shaky voice. "That's what Dad wants. He'd be overjoyed if I just stopped doing gymnastics forever. I guess you would be, too!"

"Amber, hold on a minute," her mother cried. "I'd never tell you to quit gymnastics. I know what it's like to love something that deeply. I also think it's good you've made some friends and you're spending time with them. But your father is right about one thing. School is important, particularly for someone as intelligent as you. I don't think you should quit gymnastics. But I do think you have to get more organized."

"But I've been trying!" Amber burst out.

"Well, keep trying," her mother said gently.

Amber leaned back on the couch. Get organized! Her mother sounded just like Jessica. She made getting organized sound so easy. But it wasn't. Or maybe her mother was right, Amber thought hopefully. Maybe she just hadn't given it enough time.

* * *

"Pssst!" Doug Miller tapped Amber on the

98

shoulder. "Special delivery from your pal over there!" He jerked his thumb in Chelsea's direction. Amber slid the note into her opened textbook. It usually made her nervous when Chelsea passed her notes in class. This time, however, Amber was glad. Mr. Goldman was out sick today, and their substitute teacher was Mrs. Benjamin. Having substitute teachers was sometimes kind of fun, but Mrs. Benjamin was about ninety years old. Her idea of teaching was reading textbooks out loud to them. It was fourth period English now, so Mrs. Benjamin was reading their English textbook. Amber quickly unfolded the note.

Hey, Blue Star!
We're having a team meeting (unofficial, of course). We'll meet at the second to last picnic table by the football field. (Yeah, the usual place. Boring, I know!) 12:30 p.m. Be there or else!

The note was signed with a smiley face, as usual. Amber glanced over at Chelsea and nodded. Chelsea grinned. Then suddenly Amber had an anxious thought. What if her teammates had called the meeting to tell her that if she didn't shape up they didn't want her on the team anymore?

"A comma is used to provide a short breathing space in a sentence . . . ." Mrs. Benjamin droned. Just then the bell rang. The whole class let out a huge sigh of relief.

Scooping up her books, Amber dashed out of the classroom toward her locker. She knew she should wait for Chelsea, but if the Blue Stars did have something bad to say to her, she'd rather not find out about it until she had to. Amber opened her locker and picked up her brown-bag lunch. She put on her jean jacket and jogged nervously toward the playing field.

When she got to the picnic table, Lily and Jessica were already there. Chelsea came up a moment later. "Amber, where were you?" she demanded breathlessly. "I looked for you everywhere!"

Amber shrugged. "I thought if it was a meeting I'd better get here on time," she murmured.

Jessica reached into her bag and pulled out four bottles of flavored seltzer water and four fruit yogurts. "It is a meeting, sort of. But not the kind you have to be right on time for," she said awkwardly. "Also, we brought you lunch," she gestured at the drinks and yogurts. "Go on, pick a flavor."

Amber selected a bottle of lemon-lime seltzer and a blueberry yogurt. Then Lily handed her a bagel and cream cheese neatly wrapped in plastic. "It's cinnamon-raisin," she said. "I remembered that was your favorite."

"Thanks," Amber said. She looked at Lily, then at Chelsea, then Jessica. They were all smiling. *If they're being so nice to me, they must have decided something important*, she thought. Were they going to kick her off the team right now, right this very minute?

"Uh, what's up?" She looked Jessica in the eye. To her dismay, Jessica blushed and looked away. "I mean, why are we having a meeting?" she pressed on bravely.

Jessica cleared her throat. "Well, I—I mean, we—

called you here today to . . . talk to you about . . ."

"Jessica," Lily broke in softly. "We're the Blue Stars, not the student council. Just get to the point. You're making Amber nervous."

"Okay." Jessica cleared her throat again. "Well, Amber, we wanted you to meet us here, because we're all friends, as well as teammates . . . and I owe you an apology."

"An apology?" Amber burst out. She was so relieved she almost leaped three feet in the air. "No, you don't. I—"

"Yes, I do," Jessica said firmly, as Lily and Chelsea both nodded. "Even if you did mess up yesterday, I was out of line yelling at you like that. We all have bad days—even me," Jessica added. "I once fell off the balance beam right after I got on in a big competition at my old gymnastics club. Anyway, the point is we all make mistakes. But we're a team and that means we have to stick together, no matter what. So I'm sorry." Jessica put out her hand. "Friends, okay?"

Amber grinned. "Friends," she agreed. "But you were right. I should have gotten more sleep. I just had a hard time getting everything done. You know, all my schoolwork, plus . . ."

"Yeah," Chelsea interrupted, "But that's over now. Your paper's done, and everything's back to normal, right?"

Amber slowly nodded.

"Best of all, we're back to normal, as friends and teammates," Lily added.

"Hear, hear!" Chelsea said, then she sighed. "It's too bad you missed Susan Cooper's question-and-answer session, though. You would have loved it. She was so great when she talked about learning to be a gymnast. It was totally inspiring!"

"I bet," said Amber. "But it's okay. I actually got to talk to Susan Cooper a little."

"You did?" her friends all cried.

"When?" said Jessica.

"Where?" said Chelsea.

"How?" said Lily. The four of them cracked up.

Amber swiftly described how she had run into Susan Cooper in the hallway outside the locker room. Then she had to repeat her conversation with the star gymnast word for word.

"That's awesome," Chelsea said when she was done. "You are so lucky, Amber!"

"Do you have the program with you?" asked Jessica shyly. "I'd like to see what she wrote."

"Yeah," Amber nodded. "I've been carrying it around with me everywhere since she gave it to me." She carefully pulled the program out of her backpack. Together the four girls read over Susan Cooper's words.

"Keep soaring!" said Jessica. "That's perfect."

"Yeah, it's a beautiful thing to say," cried Lily.

Amber folded up her program and put it away. "You're right, Chelsea," she said. "I am lucky—and I'm especially lucky to be part of the Blue Stars."

Chelsea grinned. "What can I tell you? The Blue Stars are the greatest." Right at that moment, the bell rang. The four girls leaped up and cleaned off the picnic table. "Back to Mrs. Benjamin's boring read-aloud class," Chelsea grumbled. "I never thought I'd say this, but I can't wait for Mr. Goldman to come back."

"Me, neither," Amber agreed. Secretly, she'd been relieved that Mr. Goldman was out sick. She was worried about getting her history paper back. But even getting a lousy grade from Mr. Goldman couldn't be worse than being bored to death, could it?

"Well, at least we have something great to look forward to," Chelsea declared.

"What?" Amber asked.

"Amber, don't tell me you forgot! You guys are all coming to my house this afternoon for the fabulous fashion fittings!"

"You mean the dresses are ready already?" Lily exclaimed.

Chelsea nodded. "Uh-huh, and they're even more fabulous than I hoped in my wildest dreams."

"Uh-oh," said Jessica. "So now we have only a week to make sure our routine is as stunning as our costumes!"

"Hey, we can do it." Lily smiled. "We're the Blue Stars!"

"Yeah," they all said at the same time. Amber was so happy that she felt like she was glowing all over. It was demanding to be on a gymnastics team. Still, Amber realized she wouldn't trade being a Blue Star for anything in the world!

CHAPTER THIRTEEN

Pushing up his glasses, Mr. Goldman smiled at the class. Most of the kids smiled back. The lunch bell was about to ring, and it had been a fun morning. They had played a word game, studied butterflies, and written a group poem. Everyone was in a good mood—including Amber.

She was all caught up on her homework. Also, yesterday's gymnastics practice had gone really well. Afterwards they had gone to Chelsea's house for the dress fittings. The dresses had turned out great. In her swirly, glittery blue dress Amber felt like a new person—older, glamorous even! She only wished Jason Bonetti could see her in it.

Amber snapped out of her daydream as Mr. Goldman rose to his feet and said, "Well, class, I finished grading your history papers. They kept me amused while I got over my cold. Anyway, I'm going to hand them back now. If you have any questions or problems, I'll be available all through lunch period."

The teacher walked around the classroom, handing out papers left and right. When he got to

Amber's desk, he stopped. "Here, Amber," he said in a low voice. "Come talk to me about this. This paper is not the best work you can do."

Amber nodded and took the paper out of his hand. Then she forced herself to peer down at it. On the top in red was a big C+. Her heart sank. She had never gotten a C+ in her life. To get it in history, her best subject, made it even more horrible.

Amber clasped her hands together. Mr. Goldman wanted her to come talk to him. She knew she owed it to her teacher to explain why her paper had been below her usual standard. But as the lunch bell rang, she also knew she just couldn't do it. She felt too ashamed. Instead, she gathered up her books and swiftly fled the classroom.

"Wait for me!" Chelsea called after her.

Amber slowed down just enough for Chelsea to catch up.

"How'd you do on your history paper?"

"Okay," Amber murmured as she shoved the paper deep into her backpack. She wanted to tell Chelsea the truth. She'd done horribly! But then Chelsea wouldn't necessarily think getting a C+ was so bad. On top of that the Blue Stars had been so nice to her about messing up at the exhibition. How would they feel if they knew that not only had she messed up their performance, but her paper as well? "How about you?"

"Not great, as usual." Chelsea's voice was bleak. "Look." She held out her paper. Chelsea had gotten a C+, too. But Mr. Goldman hadn't asked Chelsea to come talk to him. He'd just written, "I know you don't believe me, Chelsea, but you are capable of much better work."

"Mr. Goldman always says that," Chelsea sighed. "But I think he'd better just realize I'm a C student and a great gymnast."

"Not to mention a fabulous dress designer," said Lily behind them. Chelsea whirled around, then she laughed and took a bow. Amber watched her enviously. If only she could take her C+ as lightly as Chelsea did. But she couldn't. She couldn't bring herself to tell anyone—not even her friends—that she'd gotten a C+. But she'd have to tell her parents sooner or later.

"Are you pumped up for practice today?" asked Chelsea.

"Yeah, sure," Amber said quickly. "Hey, listen, I've got to go to the library and look up something. I'll catch you guys later, okay?"

The rest of the school day passed in a blur. Amber couldn't focus on anything but her C+. *Brain or brawn?* The words kept echoing through her mind. It was a question she couldn't answer.

Amber thought of how it had felt the first time she got up on the parallel bars. She'd gone swooping through the air so high and fast that it seemed as if she would never come down. She couldn't imagine not doing that anymore. And if she quit gymnastics, she would probably lose her friends, too. In a way, that was the worst thing of all.

Yet if her grades kept slipping, there was no way her father would ever let her stay on the team. Amber was still puzzling over her dilemma when the final bell rang. It was time to go to practice.

Amber had been anxious about practice all afternoon. She dreaded Mrs. Randall and her teammates watching to see if she had truly rebounded from her disastrous performance at the exhibition. But practice turned out to be a relief. Mrs. Randall put them through a grueling warm-up. In her chin-ups and push-ups Amber was able to forget her troubles for a while. Today, they were focusing on the balance beam.

Working on the beam took tons of concentration. Amber focused on her routine as she never had before. It paid off. Her leaps and saltos were higher and crisper than they'd ever been. Even Jessica was impressed, and Mrs. Randall told Amber she was making a terrific comeback. "That's what true grit is," the coach said. "Coming back from a bad performance stronger than ever."

Despite her worries, that made Amber feel proud. But once practice was over and she started home, her spirits sank again. She had to tell her parents about her paper. But how? She slowly pushed open her front door and tiptoed into the hall.

"Amber, is that you?" her father called out. Amber wondered why he was already home.

"Yeah, it's me."

"Your mom and I want to talk to you. We're in the den."

Amber took a deep breath. Her father's voice sounded suspiciously solemn. She had a feeling she wasn't going to have to worry about telling her parents about her history paper. Somehow they knew already.

Amber slowly walked back to the den. Her father and mother were sitting side by side on the old brown leather coach. Her mom looked worried, but her dad looked mad.

"What is it?" Amber asked in a quavery voice.

"I called your teacher, Mr. Goldman, today," her mom began. "I wanted to ask him about your midterm report, and he said he was glad I'd called."

"He told your mother you did very poorly on your history term paper," her father cut in. "Apparently, he's worried about you. He asked your mother and I to come in for a conference. He says your grades have been slipping. He also says you claimed there'd been trouble at home. A family emergency."

Mr. Rogers sighed. "Your mother told him we didn't know anything about a family emergency, except for your grandmother breaking her ankle. And I can't believe that's what's causing all this trouble at school. When your mother called me at work to tell me, I thought I'd come right home so we could talk. I think you'd better tell us what's really been going on, Amber."

Amber was silent for a moment. "I guess I've sort of had a hard time keeping up with everything," she began. In a halting voice she told her parents everything that had been going on. How Grandma Ida's birthday party happened the day before her history outline was due. How scared she was about turning the outline in late, and how being in the exhibition meant a lot of extra gymnastics practices. "I've also been spending more time with my friends, I guess," she added reluctantly.

"I see," her father said when she was done. Amber could tell by his expression that nothing she'd said came as much of a surprise. "Well, I don't have to tell you that I was always worried about you spending so much time on gymnastics. Now, I'm sorry to say, it's obvious that I was right."

Amber opened her mouth, but no sound came out.

"Charles," her mother cried, "you're right to a point, but . . ."

Her father held up his hand. "Cora, I know what you're going to say. I do understand that gymnastics is important to Amber. But we've always agreed there's nothing as important as our children getting a good education. It seems to me that if Amber can't keep her grades up and do gymnastics, then she's going to have to quit gymnastics. At least she's going to have to quit this team she's on."

Amber opened her eyes wide. She had been thinking about quitting the Blue Stars all day long. Yet now that her father said she should, Amber knew it was impossible.

"But, Daddy," she burst out. "I can't quit the team. We have our first real competition next week.

If I quit now, the others will never forgive me!"

Her father's expression softened. "Okay, Amber," he said. "You can stay on the team until then. After the competition you're going to have to make some hard choices. Gymnastics is fine to do for fun, but a good education lasts your whole life." Her father looked right at her. "I know it's hard, Amber, but one day you'll see I'm right about this."

"No," she heard herself say. "You're not right, Daddy. You know what I think?" she added, her voice rising. "I think you don't know me. I think you don't have any idea what's really important to me. And you don't even care about finding out. All you care about is that I do well in school and get good grades."

Her father's face fell. "But Amber . . ."

Amber didn't stay to listen. Instead, she turned and ran up to her room. She flopped on her bed and stuck her head under her pillow. Shortly, someone knocked on the door. "Go away!" she shouted.

"Come on, Amber, it's me. Let me in, please?"

"I said, go away!"

"Please open the door."

Amber sighed, got up, and opened the door for her father. He came in holding the family photo album under his arm.

"We have to talk," he said.

"Daddy, I said everything I have to say."

"You said a lot, and some of what you said was true." Her father sat down at her desk. "Maybe I don't understand what's important to you. At least, maybe I didn't realize how important gymnastics is to you. Your mom really gave me a hard time after you ran upstairs. She said I don't listen."

Mr. Rogers shook his head and smiled sadly. "Maybe she's right. I remember when I was in high school, I loved baseball more than anything. I had dreams of being a big-time ballplayer. But your grandfather made me stay in and study. He wouldn't even let me try out for the school team. I was so mad, but later I realized he was right. There was no way I was ever going to be a major league pitcher.

"Still," her father added wistfully, "I don't think it would have hurt to let me play a little. Amber, I really don't want to make you quit gymnastics against your will. But I do want to try to explain why your education is so important to me. Your mother says I just tell you kids to do things, and I don't tell you *why*."

Her dad fell silent and opened the photo album. Amber glanced at it over his shoulder. She hadn't looked at the family album in a long time. She smiled at an old black-and-white snapshot of Grandma Ida when she was a girl, standing on her head in someone's backyard. Then her eyes fell on a picture of Grandpa Henry as a young man. *He was so handsome*, Amber thought with a pang. She could hardly believe he wasn't with them anymore.

"Your grandfather was so strict with me because he wanted me to get the education he never could," her father said in a tightly controlled voice. "I don't know if I ever told you this, but your grandfather desperately wanted to be a doctor when he was young. His family had no money, though, and he didn't know much about scholarships. Your grandfather went to college for a year, but then his father got laid off and he had to drop out to help the family. That was when he joined the post office."

Amber swallowed. She'd never had any idea that her grandfather wanted to be a doctor.

"Your grandfather wanted to make sure that didn't happen to me," her father went on. "That's why he pushed me so hard—so I would be able to do whatever I wanted. I want the same thing for you, Amber. You have a good mind. I want you to use it to live your dreams. That's why I push you and Sam the way I do. Not because I don't care, but because I do. Do you understand?"

Amber nodded. "Yes, Daddy." She moved closer. Together they leafed through the rest of the album. Amber studied the faces in the photos as she never had before, thinking of all the different people in her family with all their different dreams.

"I guess what I'm saying is I want you to think hard about what your dream really is," her father said after awhile.

Amber lifted her head. "I will. And thanks for showing me the pictures, Daddy." She glanced down at a snapshot of Grandpa Henry as an old man. *He would have been a great doctor*, she thought sadly. It was too bad he never got a chance to be one. Her father was right. She had a lot of hard thinking to do.

CHAPTER FOURTEEN

Amber," Mrs. Randall called. "You're not stretching your body enough in pre-flight. That's why you're not getting enough height in your handspring. Go back and try it again." Backing up, Amber ran toward the pommel horse.

"Remember to stretch!" Amber heard Mrs. Randall shout as she soared into the air. She tried her best, and touching the horse for a brief moment, rose head over heels into her after-flight. This time Amber could tell she'd gotten a lot more height—enough to give her a rush of adrenaline. Her heart pounding, she came in for her landing.

"Nice job, Amber," Mrs. Randall said, nodding approvingly.

"Yeah!" put in Chelsea. "You looked great up there."

"I felt great," Amber replied simply. She had. It was a good thing, too, because this was the Blue Stars' last practice before their big match against Barnard. The team was really coming together, she thought with a pang. Everyone was looking good—even her.

The only problem was she didn't know how much longer she'd be on the team.

Ever since her conversation with her father, Amber had been thinking *hard*. Mostly she'd been thinking about her grandfather. She'd always assumed Grandpa Henry was a mailman because he wanted to be. But her grandfather had wanted to be a doctor. That meant he'd worked his whole life at a job he didn't really like.

Amber had thought about that all weekend. By the time Monday morning came, she had made her decision. She couldn't let what had happened to her grandfather happen to her. She had to work to make *all* her dreams come true. That meant keeping up her grades—no matter what. To do that, she'd have to quit the Blue Stars. It was the right thing to do.

Amber gazed wistfully around the drafty, barnlike gym. She couldn't imagine never standing here again, practicing the same moves over and over, with Mrs. Randall correcting her every step of the way.

Quitting the Blue Stars might be the right thing to do, but it felt all wrong.

"Hey, are you okay?" Chelsea whispered beside her.

"Yeah, sure, why?" Amber whispered back.

Chelsea shrugged. "You just looked incredibly sad for a moment." She gave Amber a big smile as Lily made her dismount. "Cheer up, okay? Don't forget what Susan Cooper wrote you: 'Whatever happens, keep on soaring.'"

"I won't," Amber mumbled. Thinking about her conversation with Susan Cooper made the idea of giving up gymnastics for good even more unbearable.

"Okay, that's enough for today," Mrs. Randall said, glancing at her watch. "We had a good workout, didn't we?"

"That's one way to put it," Chelsea moaned. "A good torture session would be more like it."

"Well, you'll be happy tomorrow." Mrs. Randall grinned. "I know I've been pretty tough on you, but the extra work on your muscles will definitely pay off in terms of strength and endurance. Now I know we're all a little anxious about tomorrow. . . ."

"That's the understatement of the year," Lily murmured.

"And so," Mrs. Randall went on, "I just wanted to say that you guys definitely look like winners to me!" Her eyes focused on Amber. "Especially you, Amber," she said softly. "You've really pulled yourself together since last week."

"Hooray," Chelsea, Jessica, and Lily all shouted.

Amber tried to smile, but she couldn't. All she could think about was that she wouldn't be on the team much longer.

"Thanks, Mrs. Randall," she forced herself to say.

"Don't thank me. You've been doing really well."

Mrs. Randall beamed at her. It made Amber feel even worse, but it also made her feel determined. This time, she promised herself, she would give a truly great performance. Then her heart sank still further.

She had promised herself that before the exhibition, and look what had happened. There was a good chance she would just blow it again.

"So get lots of rest," Mrs. Randall went on, "and tomorrow go out there and do exactly what you've been doing. Barnard's going to have a tough time against you guys!"

Everyone grinned at her. Then they went quickly to the locker room.

"Whew," said Chelsea, after they had showered and changed. "I feel prepared, but then again, I don't. You know what I mean?"

"Uh-huh," Lily nodded solemnly. "Just thinking about those tough Barnard girls gives me goose bumps."

"They are tough," Jessica agreed. "But I think the coach is right. We're a match for them. We just better make sure to do what the coach says. Eat right, get enough sleep—" She glanced over at Amber. "Oops! Sorry," she said, her cheeks turning pink. "I wasn't trying to get at you about last time, Amber, honestly. You've been doing great in practice and—"

"That's okay," Amber said. "Believe me, I plan to get plenty of sleep tonight."

Chelsea reached out and gave her a hug. "Good, but don't overdo it, all right? A normal amount will be fine. And don't worry so much. Just because things didn't go your way last time doesn't mean this time it won't work out for you."

"Yeah," said Lily. "You're going to be fabulous, Amber."

"You might even outshine me," said Jessica.

"Thanks," Amber replied. Suddenly she realized why her friends were being so nice. They thought she was upset because she was afraid she was going to mess up again tomorrow. What would they say if they knew the real reason was that she wasn't going to be a Blue Star much longer?

She picked up her backpack. "Anyway, I've got to get going. See you guys tomorrow."

Not even waiting to see if any of her friends wanted to walk with her, Amber ran out of the gym. Outside, the sky had clouded over, and Amber could hear thunder rumbling in the distance. Lowering her head, she dashed down Tillman Avenue. Yet before she'd gotten very far, fat raindrops started falling from the sky.

It hardly ever rains at this time of year, Amber thought. But somehow the rain made sense. It was as if even the weather was picking up her dismal mood. She turned up the collar of her jean jacket and started running.

"Hey," someone called. "You want to get out of the rain?"

Amber looked up. Jason Bonetti was standing in front of her, holding a giant red umbrella.

"Yeah . . . uh . . . sure." *Butterflies!* Amber thought, stepping under the umbrella.

"Where do you have to go?" Jason asked.

"Home," Amber stammered.

"So where do you live?"

"On Cedar. Two blocks off Tillman. But you don't have to take me all the way there," she added quickly.

"Hey, no problem. I don't mind making a small detour."

"Well, if you're sure . . . ."

"I can't let the local star gymnast get soaked, can I?" Jason said, with a smile.

Amber made a face. "I'm not exactly a star gymnast," she said. "I don't even know if I'm a good gymnast."

Jason looked at her. "I bet you are," he said. "I've seen the way you and your friends talk about gymnastics. It sounds like you're all pretty serious."

Amber sighed. "Yeah, but—well . . . we were in a big exhibition last week, and I totally blew it." She tried to smile. "And we have a major competition tomorrow."

"Are you worried about it?" asked Jason seriously.

Amber nodded. "Yeah," she confessed.

"Well, you seem like a pretty tough little kid," he said slowly. "I believe you can do it."

"You do?"

"Yeah," Jason smiled.

Amber lifted her head and smiled back. Then she saw that they were almost to her house. "I live in that yellow house across the street," she said, feeling flustered. "Well, bye, and . . . thanks."

"My pleasure. And good luck tomorrow. I know you're going to be great." Jason took off down the street.

Amber stared after him. Jason Bonetti was the nicest guy she had ever met. Of course, he had called her a little kid, Amber reminded herself as she started up the driveway. But he'd also told her he believed in her. That counted for a lot. In a way it was even better than if he'd said he liked her or something.

Amber grinned, then her face became serious again.

Jason Bonetti thought she could give a good performance. Mrs. Randall, Chelsea, Lily, and Jessica all thought she could give a good performance. She had to prove them right. Tomorrow, she promised herself, she was going to give the performance she had dreamed of giving at the exhibition. She had to, because it was probably the last chance she would ever get to show what she could do.

CHAPTER FIFTEEN

Amber gripped her gym bag tightly and followed Chelsea through the swinging doors that led to the Barnard gym. The polished wooden floor of the gym shone brilliantly under the lights. "Pretty ritzy," Lily muttered nervously.

"Yeah," said Chelsea. "I wish we had a place like this to practice in."

Amber had to agree. Barnard's gleaming new gymnasium was about as far as they could get from the drafty old gymnastics room on Tillman Avenue. The gymnasium stands were full of students, teachers, and parents. Amber looked around for her mom and Grandma Ida. She spotted them in the front row and gave them a tiny wave. Her teammates were waving at their families, too.

Amber swallowed. She had expected coming to Barnard to be less scary than going to the big athletics pavilion downtown, but it wasn't.

"At least they don't have those huge video monitors," sighed Chelsea, as if she was reading Amber's mind.

"Yeah," Jessica said. "But it's a smaller place. They don't need to see you two hundred times larger than life here to spot your mistakes."

The Barnard team was already warming up on the other side of the gym. They looked poised and confident in their bright red-and-white-striped leotards.

"All right," Mrs. Randall said. "Let's get limber!"

It felt strange to be warming up in front of a crowd of Barnard supporters. Amber tried to ignore the crowd, but every few seconds the whole gym rang with shouts of "Barnard! Barnard!"

At last a whistle blew and the judges came out. Then the principal of Barnard stepped forward. "Today," she said with a warm smile, "our school is competing against a brand new team. Let's give a big welcome to the Tillman Avenue Gym Club Girls' Gymnastics Team!" Most of the audience applauded politely, but a few people booed.

"Okay," Mrs. Randall said a bit anxiously. "You know the routine—each team will pick a starting event. These will be the first two events in the competition. The remaining events will follow the same order as the Olympics: vaulting, parallel bars, balance beam, and floor. You'll all get two minutes on each and no more, so watch your timing. I guess that's all. Except good luck, and I know you can do it." Their coach gave them each a quick hug.

Amber watched intently as Mrs. Randall and the Barnard coach drew straws to see what event each team would start with. The judges soon announced the results. The Blue Stars had drawn floor exercise. Barnard's team had drawn the balance beam. This meant the order in this competition would be floor, beam, vaulting, and bars.

Amber's stomach lurched. She would be beginning with the event she'd messed up so badly at the exhibition. Worse, she wouldn't get to perform in her strongest event until the very end of the meet.

Mrs. Randall gave them a nod. The group floor exercises would be first, followed by their individual routines. As "Jeremy" began to play over the Barnard P.A. system, the four Blue Stars took their places.

"One, two, three," Jessica counted off the beats. "Go!" The four girls handsprung together, then flic-flacked out in a widening circle, before coming together again and twirling around.

As she finished her last twirl, Amber leaped into her first aerial cartwheel. For once, her height was good. As Mrs. Randall would say, she almost managed to "hit the ceiling." By the time Amber ran to pick up her ribbon for the final part of the routine, she was feeling exhilarated. Maybe this time she *would* give a truly great performance!

Incorporating a rhythmic gymnastics section into a floor exercise was unusual. At first Mrs. Randall hadn't been sure it was a good idea. But Jessica had begged her to let the Blue Stars give it a try. Now it had finally paid off. All four girls managed to keep the ribbons swirling in motion. And when they were done, they could tell by the audience's reaction that the ribbon exercise had given them a spectacular finale.

When the judges posted the scores, the Blue Stars flung their arms around each other. An 8.1 for technique and an 8.6 for artistic interpretation. Those would be hard scores for Barnard to beat.

The Blue Stars watched in anticipation as Barnard took to the floor. Barnard's music was a classical piece called "Dance of the Bumblebee." The music really sounded like a bumblebee. The Barnard girls gave a terrific performance, gracefully leaping and tumbling all over the floor. In fact, the judges gave the Barnard team slightly higher scores than the Blue Stars—an 8.3 and an 8.6.

"It's not fair," Chelsea wailed in frustration. "Their routine was way easier than ours!"

Jessica sighed. "Judges always like more classical routines," she said. "I told you guys that when you decided to use Pearl Jam for the music, remember?"

"Yeah, but—" Chelsea began.

"Chill out, Chelsea," Lily advised. "They're only leading by two-tenths of a point."

Next came the individual floor exercises. The Blue Stars performed first. In rapid succession, the girls did their routines. Chelsea was a crowd-pleaser, and Jessica was fantastic as usual. Amber didn't do badly, either. But Lily lost her balance on a cartwheel and got a half-point deducted for ending her routine before her music stopped.

"Sorry, you guys," she moaned as she ran off the floor.

"Don't worry, you did fine," Mrs. Randall reassured her. But at the end of the individual floor exercises, Barnard was leading by a whole point.

They turned to watch the Barnard girls on the balance beam. Every member of the team performed well, but the star was a short red-haired girl. She was the last one up, and her routine was just about flawless. When she finished with a difficult back salto dismount, the crowd started stamping and whistling.

The Blue Stars let out a collective sigh. Then Chelsea went up to begin her routine. Amber, who was spotting, thought Chelsea did a good job, but as usual, her leg and foot placement were a little sloppy. The judges noticed. They gave Chelsea high marks for artistic interpretation, but lower marks for technique. The Barnard team was pulling further ahead!

Amber bit her lip as her name was called. Then, feeling adrenaline pump through her, she mounted the beam. All Mrs. Randall's hours of instruction filled her mind and body. *Stretch your legs, point your toes, stomach in, back arched!* The routine whipped by as if it was a dream. Amber was concentrating so hard that she was surprised when it was time for her last move—an aerial cartwheel into a round-off dismount. She threw herself forward, landing with both feet squarely on the mat. She'd nailed it! Bowing quickly, she ran to her teammates.

"Amber, that was great!" Lily cried.

"Yeah, you're really on fire today," Chelsea whooped.

"How were my scores?" Amber craned her neck, trying to see the board.

"Excellent," Jessica declared. "An 8.0 and an 8.9. That'll definitely bring us up by at least half a point. We're getting back in this!"

"Come on, Lily," said Mrs. Randall. "You're next."

"Why me?" Lily wailed. But as she went up to the beam, her chin jutted out resolutely. And by the time she was halfway through her routine, the others were cheering wildly. Lily was doing a fantastic job. Her nervousness seemed to be pushing her to a higher level of performance. Lily's natural grace truly shone through. The only sour note came at the very end. Lily was doing a round-off dismount and as she landed, she stumbled slightly.

Close to tears, Lily slunk back to her teammates. "I can't believe it," she cried. "I was doing so great and . . ."

"They didn't count it against you that much," Jessica cut in. "They still gave you a 7.0 and a 7.5."

"Yeah," said Chelsea anxiously. "But no one from Barnard got less than a 7.2!"

"Well," said Jessica, "I guess that means I'd better give a fantastic performance."

Jessica walked out to the beam and got on with a perfect springboard mount. She had to be nervous, but she wasn't showing it. Her every move was incredibly assured and graceful. Amber's eyes widened. She knew Jessica was good, but until today she had never entirely realized *how* good. Jessica did all the moves she and the other Blue Stars had practiced so long and hard, making them look as effortless as breathing.

As Jessica raced back over to them, the judges posted her scores. The Blue Stars started cheering. A 9.0 and a 9.9! They were now only 1.3 points behind Barnard!

Amber's eyes narrowed as the Barnard girls started their vaulting. She was praying they wouldn't be as good at vaulting as they were at everything else. But they were. At the end of the vaulting, despite Chelsea's best efforts, the Blue Stars were still a point behind.

There was only one event left, one chance to catch up with Barnard: the uneven parallel bars.

Jessica was to go first, then Chelsea, then Lily. Amber would perform last.

Jessica gave a solid performance, but the magic she had worked on the beam seemed to have used up her energy. Her scores were respectable, but nothing stunning. Chelsea did better and was overjoyed when the judges gave her an 8.5—her highest score ever in the event. Lily's scores were decent—a 7.0 and a 6.9, but not enough to put the Blue Stars solidly ahead.

"Okay, Amber, you're next," Mrs. Randall called.

Amber's heart thudded wildly. Her teammates eyed her. She knew what they were thinking. For the

Blue Stars to win—or even tie—Amber Rogers was going to have to give the performance of her life.

Amber bent over to chalk her hands. Then she raced up to the bars and swung on. *Remember, whatever happens, don't be afraid to keep on soaring.* Susan Cooper's words floated into her mind. She thought of what the gymnast had said, and of Grandpa Henry, and of the faded snapshot of Grandma Ida standing on her head in the family album. All the images seemed to flow around her and gather into a single driving idea. This time Amber would make herself soar on the bars as never before!

Amber swung from a long hang on the low bars up into a straddle-kip glide, then she did a clear hip circle to a handstand. Now came the hardest part of her routine: her handstand pirouette.

Amber clenched the bar, her legs stretched straight above her. Her muscles felt strong, but her will felt even stronger. She switched her hand position, pirouetted, and cast herself backward, arching her back high. Then she rose up again into her backward salto dismount. As she started her somersault, Amber flung herself up into the air—higher than she had ever done before. Down she swooped, hitting the mat with a satisfying *thud!* Suddenly she started to stumble, but she tensed her muscles and held her position. Then she flung her arms up over her head, saluting the judges.

As the crowd cheered, a smile slid across Amber's face.

Maybe she was going to have to quit the Blue Stars. Maybe her performance wasn't even going to be enough to win the match. But Amber had done what she'd promised herself she would do. She had given the best performance she knew how to give when it really counted. For once in her life, Amber had truly managed to fly. Nodding at the crowd, she ran back to her team.

Mrs. Randall hugged her tightly. "Amber!" she cried. "You were fantastic!"

"Yeah, you looked awesome," chimed in Jessica.

"Amber to the rescue!" Lily said.

"Just look at your scores!" Chelsea grinned, gesturing at the board. Amber looked. An 8.9 and a 9.3. They weren't quite up to Jessica's level, but they still gave the Blue Stars a healthy lead over Barnard. Now everything depended on how well Barnard performed.

Amber could hardly bear to watch as the Barnard team got into position in front of the bars. The Barnard girls didn't chalk their hands because they were all wearing handgrips. The first three girls did their routines. Amber began to breathe a little easier. Their scores were good, but she didn't think they were good enough to push them past the Blue Stars. The final Barnard girl stepped forward. It was the red-haired girl who had done so well on the beam.

Amber sucked in her breath as the red-haired girl swung up to the lower bar. The girl did a wide hip circle into a handstand pirouette. Amber watched, her chest tightening. The Barnard girl was good. Better than good. She was great. Her performance was as good as Amber's had been, if not better. Amber glanced at her teammates. She could tell they thought so, too.

The red-haired girl swung down from her pirouette, then up into a simple handstand with her legs together. Next, her legs scissoring apart crisply, she went into her dismount. It was a difficult dismount: a flyaway double-back dismount in tuck position. To do it right, the red-haired girl had to do two backward saltos in a tuck position, then land on the mat. Amber looked away as the girl came tumbling down. Then she heard a loud *thump!* She looked back to see the red-haired girl stumble to her knees.

"She totally blew it!" Jessica breathed. "She jumped too fast! I don't believe it! We won!" She turned and threw her arms around Amber. "Hooray!" Chelsea flung her arms around Amber, too, and so did Lily.

Amber was overwhelmed. The Blue Stars had won! She started cheering along with her teammates, then suddenly she stopped. She glanced over at the red-haired girl from Barnard. The girl was surrounded by her teammates, too, only she was hiding her face in her hands while her teammates tried to comfort her. Amber felt a twinge of sympathy for her. She knew exactly how the red-haired girl felt.

"The Tillman Avenue Gym Club's girls are the blue-ribbon winners today," the Barnard principal announced. "It was a tight match and both teams competed hard. Let's give everyone a big hand."

In a daze, Amber followed her teammates up to collect their ribbons. Then she looked into the audience. To her amazement, her father and Sam were sitting next to her mom. They had never come to watch her before. Amber waved happily. Then it hit her. It was a good thing they had decided to come, because this was probably her very last gymnastics performance ever.

As the Blue Stars started back to the locker room, tears filled her eyes.

"Hey, Amber, what's wrong?" Chelsea took her by the arm. "You shouldn't be crying now. We won, remember?"

"Yeah," said Lily. "Thanks to you. You saved us—along with Jessica, of course."

"Yeah, you were fantastic," Jessica said. "No way we could have done it without you."

Amber choked. "That's not true," she heard herself say. "You guys will be fine without me."

"What do you mean?" Chelsea demanded.

"I-I have to quit the team," Amber mumbled, turning her face away.

CHAPTER SIXTEEN

Y ou're quitting the team?" exclaimed Chelsea. "But, Amber, you can't!"

"Yeah! How can we be the Blue Stars without our fourth star?" demanded Lily.

"Why are you quitting?" Jessica asked. "It's not because of me, is it?" she added anxiously. "I know I get carried away sometimes—especially about gymnastics—but—"

"It has nothing to do with you, Jessica," Amber interrupted. "Honest." She tried to think of a way to explain to her friends why she couldn't be a Blue Star any longer. It was so complicated. Part of it was her schoolwork and part of it was her family. Grandpa Henry's face floated in front of her and she heard her father's voice saying, "He never got to live his dream."

Amber stared down at her gymnastics slippers. She and Grandma Ida had bought them the day of the Blue Star tryouts. They were well broken in now. Her chest started to ache. "I have to quit because . . ."

"I know why," Chelsea piped up suddenly. "It's your schoolwork, isn't it?" Amber looked up at her friend. Chelsea didn't sound angry or like she thought Amber was being stupid. She just sounded sorry.

"Yeah, sort of," Amber admitted. "How did you know?"

"Well," Chelsea looked sheepish, "I didn't mean to, but I saw the grade you got on your history paper that day when we were coming out of class. I felt really bad for you," Chelsea went on, "but I didn't know how to bring it up without sounding pushy. I was waiting for you to tell me about it yourself, I guess. But you didn't, and then everything got so hectic . . . . Anyway, I should have said something. I knew it was a big deal for you."

"You got a C+, too," Amber said. "I didn't try to make you feel better about it."

Chelsea shrugged. "That's different. You've heard me say a million times that I'm a born C student and stuff. But I know doing well in school really matters to you."

"And to your family," put in Lily understandingly. "Boy, do I know how that is! But I still don't see why you have to quit gymnastics. You can get your grades back up again."

Amber shook her head. "I don't know," she said. "It's pretty hard balancing everything."

"Yeah," Jessica agreed. "It's tough to concentrate on school when you're spending so much time on gymnastics. I've been having trouble keeping up with my homework, too."

Amber stared at her in surprise. She always

thought organized Jessica had everything under control. "You have?"

"Uh-huh," Jessica made a face. "I got a C on my last math test. My mom threw a fit."

"I can imagine," Amber said after a pause. "That's a big part of why I can't be on the Blue Stars anymore. My dad really laid it on the line for me."

"What did he say?" Chelsea prompted.

Amber swallowed. "He said I had to choose," she said. "You know, brain or brawn? Just like that quiz in *Snazzy*. But it was more than that." Then she described to her friends how her dad had showed her the old family album and told them the story of Grandpa Henry's life.

"It would be one thing if my dad was just being mean or something," she finished helplessly. "But he isn't. He really cares about me, and he's right in a way. My grandfather didn't get to do what he wanted. He lost his dream. I can't let that happen to me."

Her friends nodded. For a long moment no one said anything. "I understand," Chelsea said at last. "But I still think it would be totally wrong for you to quit gymnastics. I can't tell you what to do, Amber, but gymnastics is important to you. It is to all of us. I guess what I'm trying to say is that everyone has their own dreams."

"Yeah," said Lily. "You just have to find a way to make yours work better. You know, brain and brawn."

Amber sighed. "I wish I could," she said in a flat voice. "But I've tried. I don't know what more I could do to make everything work out better."

"You tried on your own," Chelsea said. "But if we all try together, maybe we can find a way. I know I haven't always been too understanding about how important school is to you. I think it's because deep down inside, I'm scared that no matter how hard I try I'll never be a great student, or even an okay student. But if we work together, maybe, just maybe, we can do it."

"How?" Amber demanded.

Chelsea hesitated. Suddenly Jessica snapped her fingers. "I've got it," she cried. "We all spend a lot of time on gymnastics, right?" Everyone nodded. "But," Jessica continued, "we also spend a lot of time just hanging out together. So all we need is to use our hanging-out time to get serious about school. We need to start a—what-do-you-call it?—support group!"

"Homework Anonymous?" Lily joked.

"Why not?" asked Jessica.

"That's a brilliant idea!" Chelsea shouted. "Instead of just getting together after practice and eating ice cream, we can get together, eat ice cream, *and* do our homework. We'll call ourselves The Blue Star Homework Club!"

"Yeah, and we can help each other stay out of homework trouble," Jessica said with a smile.

"We can also look over our schedules together," Lily suggested. "We can figure out what we have to do when and help one another plan our time. Then we can tell Mrs. Randall honestly when we can't meet for extra practice."

"Great," Chelsea nodded. "That way Mrs. Randall

can help us get organized, too." She turned to Amber, her eyes shining. "What do you say, Amber?" she asked.

Amber reached out and grabbed all her friends into a giant bear hug. "I say it could work!"

"All right!" Lily exclaimed.

"Yeah," said Jessica. "Brain and brawn!"

Amber smiled. "You guys are the best."

"So are you staying on the team?" asked Chelsea.

"Uh-huh," Amber nodded. "But I'll have to talk to my dad about it," she added, biting her lip.

Just then Mrs. Randall came into the locker room. "I figured I'd leave you guys alone for a while," she said. "I know you had some things to talk about." She glanced over at Amber. "I hope you're feeling better now, Amber," she said, "because everyone out there wants to congratulate you on your performance. I had to stop your father from bursting unannounced into the girls' locker room just now!"

"I guess I better go talk to him," Amber said to her friends. "Wish me luck," she whispered.

Picking up her gym bag, she made her way to the gymnasium. She was nervous about what to say to her father, but before she could say anything, he waved at her from across the gym.

"Amber," he called in a happy, booming voice. "Get over here. We've been waiting for you for ages."

Amber ran over to where her family was sitting. Sam grinned at her. "Nice going, Short-stuff." Amber made a face at him, then she looked up at her dad.

"That was amazing, Amber," he said, smiling at

her proudly. "I had no idea you guys were so good. I should have come to watch you last time. I should have come to watch you do gymnastics way before now."

Amber smiled. She had been all ready to tell her dad that she couldn't quit the team, that it wasn't right. Gymnastics was part of her dream, just like being a doctor was part of Grandpa Henry's. But now she saw she didn't have to. Of course, she'd tell her mom and dad about the Blue Star Homework Club. But that could wait. Right now she just wanted to celebrate.

"This occasion definitely calls for ice cream," said Grandma Ida. "Maybe even hot fudge sundaes. How about another trip to Fifty-Eight Flavors?" Her eyes twinkled at Amber.

She ducked away. "Hey, Dad?" she asked shyly. "Is it okay if I, uh, I ask my friends to meet us there? I mean, if they aren't doing anything else?"

"Sure," her father said. "In fact, tell them we'll buy them all ice cream."

Amber nodded and ran back across the gym toward her friends. "Fifty-Eight Flavors," she called. "My dad's buying."

Chelsea laughed. "My mom said she was buying."

"Well, I'm not eating two ice creams," said Jessica, "even if we did just have a big win."

"My dad said he was buying, too," Lily told her mischievously. "So if you don't watch it, you might just find yourself eating three."

The four girls burst out laughing.

CHAPTER SEVENTEEN

Amber stared at herself in amazement. Chelsea had promised she was going to make Amber look like a new person, but Amber hadn't expected her to do such a good job. Amber's hair was brushed out and gelled so that it fell in ringlets around her face. Chelsea had also put some makeup on her. Nothing too wild—just some cherry lip gloss, a little blush, and a touch of blue mascara.

Amber blinked at her reflection. Her blue eyelashes shimmered at her. So did the dress Chelsea and her mom had made for her. Amber was totally transformed. "Wow," she said weakly.

"Hey, you look gorgeous," Lily told her.

Amber smiled at her. "Well, I feel strange." She glanced around at her friends. They were all dressed up in their new dresses, too, and they all looked beautiful and different than they usually did. Not as different as she did, though. "Are you guys absolutely sure I don't look too fancy or something?"

"No, I mean, yes!" her friends all said at the same time.

"But this mascara," Amber persisted. "It's so flashy."

"Amber," Jessica batted her eyelashes at her. "Chelsea talked me into wearing blue mascara, too, so don't you dare take it off. I don't want to be the only one at the dance with blue eyelashes!" Chelsea and Lily both had on green mascara to match their eyes.

"Anyway," piped up Chelsea with a mischievous grin, "there's no time to change anything now. It's already seven-fifteen."

The four girls rushed downstairs and out to the driveway, where Mr. Higa was waiting in the family's ancient blue station wagon. Mr. Higa stepped out of the driver's seat to open the doors for them. "Allow me," he said. "I feel like I should wear a chauffeur's hat. You girls look like movie stars."

"Dad, we do not!"

"We are stars, though," Lily giggled.

Amber didn't say anything. She was too excited. *I feel like a movie star,* she thought as she slid into the back seat. The shimmery blue material winked up at her. She had been afraid her dad wouldn't let her go to the dance. But to her surprise, he'd been really pleased for her.

Amber peered out the window as Mr. Higa pulled up to the school doors. There were Christmas tree lights strung over the doors. Amber grinned. The school looked as dressed up as she was.

"I'll be here at nine o'clock to pick you girls up," Mr. Higa said. "Don't be late. And have a really good time."

"Don't worry, we will," Chelsea said.

She swept up the stairs with the other Blue Stars behind her. As the four girls walked down the hall to the gym, Jessica said, "Once we get inside, we're supposed to introduce ourselves to the band, right, Chelsea?"

Chelsea nodded. "Uh-huh. They're going to introduce us, and put our 'We Are the Future' tape on. Then we do our stuff. It's pretty straightforward."

"Yeah," Jessica said anxiously. "I wish we had a few more days of practice, though. The basic routine is solid, but we still aren't nailing the switch-leaps perfectly. We have to—"

"Jessica." Lily gave her a quick hug as they came up to the gym. "Relax, okay? Most of the kids watching don't even know what a switch-leap looks like. They just want to see something fun."

"Yeah," said Chelsea, grinning. "Even if we do something dumb like fall on our faces, they won't mind."

"In fact," said Lily, "they'll probably love it. The Blue Stars' flip-flop!"

"We better not," said Chelsea. "Now let's go already!" She pushed them through the open gym doors.

"Hey, Blue Stars, over here," a familiar figure waved at them from the bandstand. Amber's eyes widened. It was Jason Bonetti!

She moved closer to Chelsea. "What is Jason Bonetti doing here?" she demanded.

Chelsea grinned. "Oops! I forgot to tell you. Remember the band, The Zoom, I told you would be playing tonight? Well, Jason Bonetti is their drummer."

"And you *forgot* to tell me?" Amber squeaked.

"Well, I didn't want to make you more nervous than you might be already," Chelsea said.

"You mean you forgot accidentally on purpose," Amber exclaimed, pretending to be mad.

"Well, at first it was on purpose. Then I just forgot," Chelsea admitted. "Anyway, aren't you glad he'll get to see the fabulous new Amber Rogers?"

Amber shrugged. "Not really," she fibbed.

"You are, too! Now come on. We have to talk to him whether you want to or not." Chelsea yanked Amber toward the bandstand.

Jason smiled as they came up. "Hi, Amber," he said. "How did the competition go?"

"Great," Amber replied. "And thanks again for saving me from getting soaked." Her friends stared at her, and Amber realized she had forgotten to tell them about Jason walking her home.

"No problem," Jason said. "I'm glad the competition went so well. I knew you could do it." Then he turned and told Chelsea how the band would introduce the Blue Stars.

"Amber, what was that all about?" Chelsea asked as Jason walked back up to the bandstand.

"Nothing," Amber tried to sound casual. "Jason happened to have an umbrella, so he walked me home from practice. You know, the day before the competition, during that big thunderstorm?"

"Ahhh," said Lily.

"And you forgot to tell us about it?" Chelsea grinned. "Now who's talking about forgetting accidentally on purpose?"

"Hey, guys, I hate to cut short this fascinating discussion," Jessica broke in, "but we're on."

Amber drew in her breath as Jason walked up to the microphone and said simply, "Let's give a big hand to the greatest gymnasts around—the Blue Stars!"

The four girls glanced nervously at each other as Vanessa began to sing the first lines of "We Are the Future." Then Chelsea led them off as they had planned with a handstand-backward salto combination. The other three followed her, flashing across the gymnasium floor. Jessica had worried about them having no mats, so she hadn't incorporated too many dangerous moves into their routine. Still, as they leaped and tumbled, Amber could tell that to the kids watching, it didn't matter. The Blue Stars were blazing around the gym like bright shooting stars. It was totally the right image for her and her friends, Amber decided. Being a gymnast was kind of like being a shooting star. You had to be strong and shine bright. *Also*, Amber thought happily, *shooting stars are the only stars that truly fly across the sky!*

As she landed after her final somersault, Amber looked around the darkened gym. All her classmates were applauding wildly.

The Blue Stars wound their way through the cheering crowd to the refreshment table. "That was awesome!" Doug Miller shouted as he ran up to them.

"Yeah, you guys should call yourselves the Incredible Blue Stars," called out Chris Haskell. He smiled at Lily. "Pretty good stuff, Jackson. Save me a dance."

Amber turned to look at Lily. "I thought he never paid any attention to sixth graders!" she said.

Lily shrugged. "I met him at one of June's ballet performances," she mumbled, looking embarrassed. "It turns out his mom teaches ballet, and he's a big ballet fan." Lily grinned. "Who knows? Maybe the fact that Chris Haskell loves ballet so much will make me appreciate all June's practicing more."

"Maybe," said Amber wisely. "But I doubt it."

"Time for a toast," said Jessica. She filled four cups with bright red punch and handed one to each of her friends.

"To the Blue Stars!" said Chelsea, raising her punch glass.

The others raised their glasses, too.

"Quick, everyone make a wish," cried Lily as they clinked the plastic glasses together.

Amber hesitated. What should she wish for? A picture flashed in her mind of herself all dressed up in a glittering white leotard. She was taking a bow in front of a wildly cheering crowd. An announcer's voice trilled, "Let's hear it for our newest U.S. gymnastics gold medalist, Amber Rogers, for her amazing performance on the uneven parallel bars!" Amber blushed. Maybe it was a good wish, but it seemed a one in a million chance that it would ever really happen. Maybe instead she should just wish that she and the other Blue Stars stayed friends forever.

Amber pulled her glass toward her and took a sip of her punch.

"So what did you wish?" Chelsea asked beside her.

"Don't tell," Jessica cut in quickly. "If you tell, your wish won't come true."

"I think it'll come true," Amber said. "At least I hope so." She smiled at her friends and raised her glass again. "To you guys. The best gymnasts and the best friends I ever had."

Chelsea grinned. "We make a pretty decent team, don't we?"

"Decent?" said Jessica in mock indignation. "The Blue Stars are the best!"

"Yeah," seconded the others solemnly as they all traded high-fives.

Blame It on Chelsea

Is fearless Chelsea headed for a fall?

The Blue Stars are in a championship race! Then Chelsea injures her leg trying to perform a daring move on the balance beam. Now Chelsea can't get the fall out of her mind. Every time she gets near the beam, she breaks out in a cold sweat.

The Blue Stars have to get a substitute gymnast to fill in. They tell Chelsea they can't wait to have her back, but Chelsea's not so sure. Do the Blue Stars blame her for her reckless stunt? And will they ever forgive her if she can't conquer her fears to perform in the championship?

0-8167-3978-1

Available wherever you buy books.

Troll